THE MEADOWDALE COMMUNITY PROJECT

BY: MATT SHEA

"The Meadowdale Community Project," by Matt Shea. 978-1-62137-604-0 (Softcover) 978-1-62137-606-4 (eBook)

Library of Congress Control Number: 2014916392

Published 2014 by Virtualbookworm.com Publishing Inc., P.O. Box 9949, College Station, TX 77842, US. ©2014, Matt Shea. All rights reserved. No part of this publication may be reproduced, stored in a retrieval system, or transmitted in any form or by any means, electronic, mechanical, recording or otherwise, without the prior written permission of Matt Shea.

Manufactured in the United States of America.

THIS BOOK IS DEDICATED TO
Renée Lynn Klause

Renée Klause having a great Christmas with her kids, Dolly, Mork and Chelsey.

Renée Klause is a special friend from Heaven who greatly inspires me.

This novel that you are about to read personifies her life. It's all about the stigma society often renders to its disadvantaged. An injustice that leaves a trail of underfunded programs and segregation.

Renée Klause has lived on both the receiving end as well as the giving. When she receives assistance in any way; she immediately *gives back* in greater numbers. This ranges from assisting at the local clothing drive for the needy and their lunch program; to being heavily involved with her church and the many charitable aspects it's involved with.

Renée has helped with this book project by expressing ideas and taking pictures. She even included her wonderful golden retriever, *Dolly*. A family member who recently had to be laid down.

When I initially met her, I wondered if she ever stopped smiling. Renée is a happy soul and for good reason. Her faith in God carries her through life rain or shine.

If anyone wants to contact this angel; I will forward all messages meant for her via my website.

www.mattsheabooks.com

Renée; it's people like you who make this world a better place. I hope you enjoy this book: *It's you!*

Your special friend,

–Matt

Renée Klause with her famous golden retriever, Dolly and special friend, author Matt Shea

CONTENTS

INTRODUCTION

A delivery of recyclable material sat on a desolate loading dock. Metal banding secured a conglomeration of worn-outdated parts that once outfitted the latest county building being demolished.

It was a sign of the times. Temporary jobs were created, but only to confirm the loss of others. Crews were employed to erase the condemned structures that once housed social workers, youth counselors and senior services. These were buildings that could no longer be funded for new codes with invaluable programs falling to the wayside.

The demolition crews worked with the understanding that they could in turn create more jobs. They accepted the arduous task of separating anything recyclable and reducing it to bite-size pieces. Once this was accomplished it would be strapped on pallets and relayed to its next station: The Meadowdale Community Center, often referred to as the "MCC."

The Meadowdale Community Center was one of controversy and errant decisions. In its glory days, it was a lavish retirement home on beautifully landscaped acreage. Trails that led to picnic tables, ponds and open pastures promised a calming effect for those who lived there. The day came when the one-story wooden building with white paint and forest green trim was outdated.

From there it became the *Alcatraz Island* of Meadowdale. The desolate campus seemed to offer everything; but for what purpose? It started its second life as a youth center with a

i

gymnasium under construction. Abruptly, the project ran out of funding and was stopped with only the steel frame standing. The abandoned structure lay idle for two years until it became an overflow lot for the city's Water Department and heavy equipment. In time, it was boarded up again and subject to demolition.

A small group of local activists successfully lobbied to save the aging building and have it resurrected one last time. The landmark with the sagging back would finish out its career to serve the local handicapped and mentally challenged. An ingenious pairing that would house the city's abandoned complex with their shuffled disadvantaged.

This was where Chase Mansfield and his friends would rummage through the rusted nails, twisted metal and bent pipes; allocating them into their prospective recycle barrels. With supervision, they had free range to use anything they saw fit for artwork. This project gave the illusion that these spirited souls were playing an *important* role for the township. To many, this suggested that Chase and his friends were at best a *third wheel* for the taxpayers.

Nothing could be further from the truth.

These humble beings were blessed by their simplicity and never lost sight about caring for others. Their so-called 'limitations' never served as a barrier when they united for a cause. The unwanted material placed before them seemed to represent their lives. They *knew* there was an important use for it and with their love, courage and creative minds would find it. Their efforts would make it just as good as before, if not better.

The result?

A product that would start a trend in the town of Meadowdale. One that created pride and *did* things for others...

CHAPTER I

C hase Mansfield's breath vaporized in the morning chill. The fall weather forced the fifteen-year-old with curly blonde hair to once again bundle-up. Wearing a zipped-up blue nylon ski jacket with a matching green/blue knitted beanie he gazed at the path before him. Intense crystal blue eyes peered down the trail, spotting a familiar wooden structure. A smile of anticipation arose from the mentally disadvantaged teen as he continued his trek. Chase walked to the clearing that exposed the backside of 'portable # 3' on the campus of the MCC.

Eagerly, the lean boy who stood six-foot even approached the abandoned classroom, just shy of its outdoor electric meter.

The glass bubble that was almost six inches in diameter was conveniently eye-level for Chase to marvel at. The transparent shield enclosed a series of five penny-size one-handed 'clocks' that rotated opposite of the one next to it. There were lengthy numbers that included letters from the alphabet that were perfectly centered throughout the metal face that held the meters. Directly in the middle of this electronic gismo was a disk that lay flat with a small portion of it exposed. It slowly spun like a CD disc, showing that someone or something was still being accommodated. The conscientious boy gleamed with excitement realizing that everything checked out.

Chase Mansfield was following his daily routine whenever he attended the community center. It was now time to address his first chore of the day. Reaching into his right coat pocket, he grabbed a peanut that was still in its shell. Looking at the metal pole that ran through the utility box, he followed it to the ground. Leaning next to it was a plastic light blue bowl filled with water. Inches away was a small hole burrowed in the dirt that channeled under the obsolete building.

This hole was where a special friend lived. One that he thought about every day and fed whenever possible. It was the home of a maimed squirrel he named, *Humphrey.*

Chase pinched the peanut with his thumb and index finger while cautiously leaning over the hole. Meticulously, he positioned the nut and dropped it into the sloped opening and watched it roll downward out of sight.

Next he quietly stood up and took several steps backwards. The caretaker grabbed another nut and with a gentle underhand toss, had it land two feet away from the water bowl. Chase continued to walk backwards and grabbed a few more nuts out of his pocket, placing them into his left hand. Finally he stopped an acceptable thirty feet away from the power meter and waited.

Within a minute, a lovable squirrel with distinction made its presence known. It had an unmistakable chopped tail that resembled a wire brush that one would use to clean a pipe. It also had a clearly visible tattered left ear, confirming identification. It was definitely Humphrey as it/*he* stood up with its/*his* small arms dangling.

Chase smiled in relief. He loved Humphrey and personally appointed himself to take care of *him.* The youth maintained the distance needed for his pet to comfortably gather the food.

The rodent's nose started to twitch, utilizing senses to survey the environment. The parameter would soon be inspected at a more in-depth level. With eyes wide-open, its head began to swivel in an on/off manner like a robot. Specific angles were addressed that encompassed the native. With caution, the deformed animal lowered itself and scurried towards the awaiting treat that lay before it. There was no time to waste as the wild pet crouched in front of the peanut and using both paws, placed it into its mouth. Instantaneously it turned around and scampered back into its hole.

One-by-one, Chase began throwing peanuts towards the water bowl until his supply was empty. Soon the squirrel was back gathering the nuts and returning home with the bounty. Chase savored the moment envisioning his friend partaking on an Easter egg hunt. The imagery generated a warm feeling inside knowing that he once again took care of him. There was also a special connection he felt with Humphrey: It was as if each could relate to the other, knowing they had much in common.

———————

The doors for the MCC were open with a full day of activities waiting for Chase and his many friends. Chase wanted to be sure not to miss out on any of the fun and waved "Bye-bye" to his furry friend. The enthused boy was having his day off to a good start and walked back to the trail that led him there. His mind was racing as he focused on the next chain of events to come. Weather usually decided on what projects the community center would do on a given day. The youth looked up to see what tell-tale signs the sky would give. Clear skies indicated better odds that they would be outside. This often meant combing the community and picking up garbage for recycle. Such ventures always promised interaction with grateful neighbors and a picnic where they saw fit.

Cold temperatures suggested that art class would fill their time and be guaranteed if it rained or snowed. Either way, Chase enjoyed every minute he spent at the community center. The boy noticed gray clouds above him. His face contorted in wonderment as he thought about the many possibilities that could make up his day. He exited the short path that linked to the parking lot. There before him stood a faded white building with forest green trim. It was accompanied by a matching knee-high sign that read: Meadowdale Community Center.

This was Chase Mansfield's *home away from home.* A dilapidated structure that lost its battle against the elements years ago. A place that was once frequented by the upper crust and the 'talk of the town.'

If one took a deep breath and stood back, the aura of desperate souls would make their presence known. Decaying walls and fences were mended by emotional strokes of donated paint. They were adorned by multicolored names, personalized art and hand prints that resurrected the building's pride for a final time. A deteriorating ceremonial process that kept pace with its dysfunctional tenants.

To most it was a burial ground for lost causes. A forgotten place hidden by overgrown trees and bushes.

———————

A familiar voice called out from the distance getting Chase's attention. "Well, aren't you even going to say, "Hi" to us?" Chase immediately looked at the front doors of the complex and saw the spirited team of Renée Klause and her Golden Retriever, Dolly. They paused to acknowledge him before entering the building.

Renée Klause was a middle-aged volunteer that always had a smile on her face. She was short in stature and had lively red flowing hair with dynamic green eyes. The woman and her faithful companion, Dolly were classic examples when it came to 'making a difference.' She was handicapped and on social security, but lived to *give back.*

Her outlets ranged from her church, woman's ministry, woman's choir; to helping at the local soup kitchen, clothing drive and whatever she could be at the community center. Dolly always accompanied her and even assisted when possible. It was common to see the dog wearing a saddle bag full of treats and other supplies to help Renée with her many causes. Chase loved being close to Renée because she always gave encouragement and made him feel *good* about himself.

The teen raised his right arm and waved at the duo. He laughed for joy knowing that it was now guaranteed to be a great day at the community center! Renée waved back as Dolly barked, wagging her tail frantically. "We'll see you inside, Chase," said Renée

"Okay," responded Chase.

Renée and Dolly entered the center with Chase moments behind.

4

CHAPTER II

C hase Mansfield opened the main door to the Meadowdale Community Center. Upon entering, he was surrounded by multicolored walls and artwork he and his classmates created. The surroundings expressed how *his* culture felt by communicating through their choice of colors and illustrations. Chase and his friends were always proud whenever anyone came to visit.

Suspense was starting to mount as he walked down the hallway of the non-stop kaleidoscope. The boy was seconds away from entering the homeroom for the Special Needs Division. Here, Chase would see who he would be spending his day with and what events lay ahead.

There was a bit of swagger to Chase Mansfield's walk as he neared the homeroom. He was that 'popular guy' on campus.

His initial step into the room caused an avalanche of greetings. The role model was taken by the reception and gazed side-to-side taking inventory of his friends. As always, everyone sat in a large circle with wheelchairs, walkers, an occasional dog and smiles gracing the room.

Lois Sexton was there; a *cool* friend that was approaching her eighties and 'fit as a fiddle.' Chase knew that Lois never attended the community center without bringing a batch of her famous chocolate chip cookies. He looked to the far corner of the room where a card table traditionally stood with tantalizing refreshments. The cookies were there along with other treats.

The unmistakable cupcakes from Ella Ray's kitchen covered an entire plate. They ranged from chocolate frosting to vanilla and had a tiny American flag on top of each. Chase didn't have to look far to see Ella nodding back at him. With gusto, she extended her hand and gave her patented 'peace sign.' The late-model *hippy chick* from another generation always made things fun.

There was more on the table. Renée's home-made carrot cake, pictures of orange juice, grape juice, paper plates, cups, plastic utensils and napkins awaited.

Chase continued to survey his surroundings. His friend Justin Rodriguez sat in his motorized wheelchair next to his mother, Maria. The thirteen-year-old boy from South America was stricken with MS. His condition, however, never prevented him from being active and happy. Justin always had a smile for Chase and often did things with him off campus. His mother, Maria was a very charitable person who constantly gave her free time to the community.

Nineteen-year-old Allen Smith was making his usual faces as a way to make Chase laugh. When their eyes met, Chase busted out laughing. Allen was an easy-going guy that knew how to create fun wherever he went. He was a graduate from Meadowdale High School the year before and liked to help others. His dad, Steve sat next to him with competing facial expressions. Steve happened across The Meadowdale Community Center a few years earlier and grew attached to it. Together, the father and son team made frequent visits, helped where needed and made friends for life.

There were more present consisting of seniors, counselors, neighbors and others considered disadvantaged. Each made a friendly jest as he waved back.

At that moment, his eyes met with the person who drove him to the MCC that morning; his mother, Julia. Years ago they were abandoned by his father. This devastating blow would prove to have a silver lining. It made them stronger and fueled their propensity to stand up for justice. Julia was the most important person in Chase's life. For Julia, it was the other way around.

The thirty-eight-year-old woman with shoulder-length brown hair stared at her son. Brown eyes glowed through wire-rimmed glasses, personifying her intellect. She was obviously mild-mannered with a medium build and stature to match. Her spirit, however, could move a mountain! She was raising a boy with high standards, having accomplished the most important task:

He was proud of who he was.

Chase Mansfield was feeling at home, spotting a reserved seat next to his mom. The son hung his cap and jacket on a nearby coat rack and sat next to her.

"Well," addressed Renée Klause in a humorous tone. "We're happy to see that you could make it today, Chase." The room erupted with laughter joined by the barking of a happy Golden Retriever.

Chase laughingly rolled with the punch. "I'm glad to be here," he replied.

"Okay, Chase," she responded. Renée was this day's volunteer chairman (chairwoman) and would say the words everyone wanted to hear.

Continuing, she stood up with everyone knowing what she was about to say. "Do you know what?" she asked the room as suspense mounted. Her hands were now behind her back as she hobbled around the floor like an old man. With a gleam in her eye, she carefully looked suspiciously at everyone. All at once she jumped up with enthusiasm announcing, "It's social time!"

"Yea!" screamed out the entire room.

'Social time' was an early morning gathering designed to help everyone get better acquainted. It was the community's way to let newcomers feel welcomed. Pastries, beverages and smiles enticed introductions that blossomed into friendships. This was *their* idea of a cocktail party.

Julia grabbed Chase's hand and made a subtle motion. She communicated a message that only *he* would understand. The *old* Chase used to rush to the dessert table to be first in line. This assured him that he got what he wanted. A selfish act. His mother recently sat down with him and thoroughly explained to the boy about respecting others. Tears came from his eyes upon realizing that he was actually hurting his friends. The boy apologized to his mother and vowed never to place himself before others again.

Social time was just underway. As usual, Chase Mansfield was the first to get up, but only to walk away and allow everyone else to come first. Julia smiled at her hero as she clapped her hands in silence. The son felt good inside having his mother's approval and nodded his head with the understanding. Everyone else noticed the extra consideration Chase was giving and volleyed back.

Lois Sexton just happened to be sitting closest to the refreshment table and found herself first in line. She and the others couldn't help notice how considerate Chase was being and decided to reward him for it. Looking at the boy Lois said, "Chase, you are such a gentleman to all of us." The room all heard what she said and clapped their hands out of respect. Chase blushed as his mother raised both fists in victory. "In fact," said Lois. "I think that I will get your treats first and leave them right here on the table for you." The senior picked up a paper plate and carefully selected samples of each treat and placed the plate on the far corner of the table. Next she asked him what he'd like to drink.

"Grape juice," he replied. Lois poured grape juice into a paper cup and along with a napkin and plastic utensils, placed them by Chase's awaiting plate.

"There," said Lois. "See what you get for being so kind?"

"That's because he deserves it," commented Ella.

"He certainly does," agreed his mother. One-by-one the entire room expressed how Chase always cared about others. They were right.

Within fifteen minutes, everyone had their treats. From there, they sat in different seats joining conversations with those they wanted to get closer to. When it was all over Chase continued with his class. He began to pick up all of the garbage with Allen jumping in. Last, he wiped down the food table and returned to his chair.

All were now seated with eyes on Renée "Thank you so-much, Allen and Chase," she said. "We appreciate the extras you do for all of us." The two nodded in acknowledgment. Changing her tone, the chairperson was about to address an issue that was of importance.

"I have something *very* important to discuss with you today," said Renée as she addressed the 'Special Ed' students. Giving consistent eye-contact to Chase and his disadvantaged classmates, she got more in-depth. "As you already know, the town of Meadowdale needs our help."

That was music to their ears as they sat up like military pilots at a briefing. Renée continued her professional presentation. She made them fully aware of the *important* role they played for the community.

Renée Klause explained to them that another shipment of valuable recyclable goods was delivered to the complex. It was now time to do their part of the relay with everyone rising to their feet. Renée and Dolly guided the crew out of the room, down the hallway and to the loading dock.

Once inside, Renée opened up a locker that held safety gear provided by the state. Bright orange vests with matching hard hats were handed out to all present. Next, safety glasses and earmuffs were issued. Even Dolly wore the standard hat, vest, glasses and earmuffs. The obedient canine was then tethered to a leash so that she could watch at a safe distance.

Everyone was now in compliance with the state's safety regulations. Allen knew what had to be done next. He began to pull on the galvanized chain that would raise a rolling metal door, exposing the loading dock. Allen started to pull on the chain as the barrier inched skyward. The others watched in anticipation as the mechanical wall rolled into a cylinder above the doorway. Once finished, he secured the chain on a sturdy hitch that held the door in place. The loading dock was now exposed with a delivery waiting for the MCC Special Needs Division.

The group stayed back watching Allen follow the procedure. The adult male walked up to a pallet jack and moved the pallet inside, near the recycle bins. He put the jack away and lowered the bay door to safely conceal the dock's four-foot drop. Last, he used a pair of banding cutters to cut the metal straps from the pallets and placed them into a recycle bin labeled 'metal.'

Chase and his friends were now free to roam. With curiosity, they surrounded the unwanted configuration that also needed a home.

What they saw was crude metal pipes intertwined with old sheet metal. It was accented with aluminum conduit protruding frayed wires that reached out like crow's feet. The mound was balanced-out with rusted screws, nails and bolts sprinkled about like nuts on a sundae. To them it was a beautiful work of art that told a story. It was as if it were a lost friend from another defunct social program crying out for new life.

"Well," said Renée "We might as well get started."

Chase noticed his mother looking back in admiration. Her *man* was needed, and it was time for him to start work.

CHAPTER III

Across town a plan was in the making. It was election year, with Mayor Warren Striker sitting on the edge of his desk calculating an early campaign strategy. Holding up a section of The Meadowdale Review, he gazed at a picture of Peter Constantine. It was a paid advertisement that announced his candidacy for mayor.

Positioning his plump frame he held the print close to his face and read about the man. Scanning through his many achievements, he began to read about Peter's origin."Why, he isn't even from here," he uttered to himself. "If that's my opponent," he lashed out, "we've already won!" Throwing the paper down he looked up to his aide and nephew, Paul Blades. "It's always important to get the retired military on your side," said his uncle Warren. "Once you get them, you're practically guaranteed to win the election." In victory, the mayor raised his silver hook.

Forty-eight-year-old Warren Striker had his right hand amputated years ago when he was a soldier. The man with a mustache who stood at five-foot-eight inches always felt that he needed distinction to give him an edge in life. He requested a pirate-type hook when the surgeons replaced his hand; a counterweight offsetting the emotional scar of having never lived up to his father's expectations. It also served as a novelty that carried him far with voters who assumed the incident occurred on the battlefield. A story that was greatly distorted at a local bar during happy hour. One that had nothing to do with a motorized can opener during kitchen detail.

Twenty-year-old Paul Blades praised his uncle. The former high school football star towered over him, but viewed his idol as a giant. The husky young man with 'Striker bushy hair' always took his advice as gospel. "I get it!" he exclaimed.

The mayor winked back in approval. He leaned forward sliding off the polished wood with his feet landing on the floor. Walking around the desk, he opened a drawer and pulled out a flat veteran's hat that opened like a wallet. He positioned it on his head and stood up at attention, saluting his nephew. "And now," said the cagey mentor. "It's time to visit my dear friends at the Veteran's Hall." Paul was impressed and saluted back.

Panning back one would notice the many pictures, portraits and campaign posters displayed strategically throughout the entire office. All were of *the man with the silver hook*. Celebrities, business managers, scout leaders and other notable members of society were captured being happy with the shiny curve ever-so present. These illustrations somewhat resembled the famous Pittsburgh Steeler helmet: it was up-most important to make sure the picture was taken from the proper angle.

———————

Not far from the Mayor's office was The Meadowdale Woman's Society. Today was their monthly tea party with a special guest invited: Peter Constantine.

Peter was a naturalized citizen of Bavarian descent who wore an eye patch from the last century. The former European soldier who fought decades ago was cursed by sharing an amazing resemblance to 'Hogan's Heroes' *Colonel Klink*. The retired high school teacher was scarred, having heard every joke imaginable. The gracious man loved this country and the town he lived in. Recently, he decided to run for mayor as to further serve the community. Peter Constantine was a gentleman.

"Would you like some more tea, Mr. Constantine?" asked seventy-year-old Mildred Fawn.

"Please call me, Peter," he said with his charming voice. "And yes, I would love some more tea." The morning was graced with Peter's presence. He sincerely cared for each and every lady he visited and greatly contributed to their conversation.

"Did someone mention roses?" asked the sixty-six-year-old man. "My mother had the most beautiful rose garden in our village," he said with a tear in his eye. The woman's circle took a sip of tea and leaned forward as he began to tell a story about his childhood. "Many years ago my mother..."

Anyone who met Peter admired his compassion and wanted to get closer. "Peter," called out eighty-one-year-old Josephine Gregg, "Would you like to join in our knitting circle this afternoon?"

"I would love to," he remarked in an apologetic tone. "But I feel that I should attend a town meeting at the Veteran's Hall today." The woman's group was further taken by Peter. It was obvious that he genuinely cared about the people in Meadowdale. He was the candidate that was *asked* to run for office.

The mayoral candidate finished his tea. "It has been wonderful visiting with everyone this morning," he said. "I hope we get to do this again soon." Peter stood up and extended his arms to embrace each member. A warmth generated throughout the room intensifying the bond already created. "I have to leave now ladies," he said.

"Good-bye, Peter," cried out the many voices he touched that morning. "Please come back and see us."

The man from the Rhine went to the coat rack. Reaching in, he grabbed his coat and put it on. Next he lifted his European hat from the shelf, turned around and bowed his head. Cheerfully, the man of the hour promised to return as he waved to his fanfare. Once outside he placed the Gray hat offset with the tiny feather on top of his shiny head. Peter started to walk toward The Meadowdale Veteran's Hall. A trek that would inadvertently place him on a collision course with one Warren Striker.

Peter approached the property that displayed cannons from past wars. Traditional white rocks outlined the antique artillery and graced walkways leading to the front doors. A well-manicured yard with the ever-present American flag waved in the breeze giving a final touch. This patriotic one-level building from the 1950s stood in the very center of town. Pride was ever-present showing fresh white paint with red and blue trim.

It was almost eleven o'clock as Peter walked the gravel path that led to the hall's entrance. Inside awaited various members of the community that came to share lunch, socialize and discuss the town's future. It was an informal 'come as you are' gathering with a self-serve potluck buffet assembled.

Among those present was Mayor Warren Striker who just happened to *drop by* wearing his commemorative veteran's hat. The man with a vibrant personality approached each person like a professional caddy: he knew when to use what club. Egos were massaged with every joke counter-punched. The 'life of the party' was encouraged to stay for lunch. He accepted the offer noticing that the most senior vets were already in the buffet line.

Warren followed suit and joined the procession by grabbing a paper plate with some napkins and plastic utensils. Mounting salad, mashed potatoes, fried chicken and other goodies on his plate, he hobnobbed with the elite. Once done, he sat at the most popular table where all could see.

Warren Striker was in true form being *one of the guys.* Despite being surrounded by machine gunners, pilots and Purple Hearts; he did his best to keep his end up. A story from the trenches would be told with Warren trying to reciprocate on an even playing field. On occasion, he would be interrupted by a senior who would lean back in his chair asking, "How old are you?"

Between stories, a lean figure in the buffet line caught his attention. It was a seemingly mild-mannered man who had a bald head and an unmistakable eye patch. It was clearly the man he read about in the paper earlier that day: his adversary Peter

Constantine. A concerned Warren Striker began to size-up his opponent with round one about to unfold.

The war stories continued with the mayor keeping an eye on Peter's every move. The incumbent couldn't help but notice how attentive Peter listened to others and laughed along with a good story. It was obvious his opposition had a class about himself that complimented everyone.

Lunch eventually dwindled down to Styrofoam cups filled with coffee and napkins holding pastries. Everyone was free to roam and like musical chairs; formed new circles. Warren Striker got his dessert and nonchalantly positioned himself in the same group as Peter. Charles Bentley, a highly decorated WWII veteran also joined in. Warren loved the situation knowing the feeble old man with a walker served his duty on the European campaign. A nice trump card to use against a Bavarian man with one eye.

Once the gathering was established, Warren initiated a conversation. "That's a very nice ad I saw in the paper this morning," he commented to Peter with all his charm. "You would do a great job serving this town."

Peter Constantine was flattered. "Mayor Striker, let me explain," he said in an apologetic tone. "I was asked by the school board to run because of the views we share. My goal is to simply address those who are usually quiet around election time and get them more involved." Peter continued, "You are doing a fine job, and I never felt that I'd actually be elected."

That answer greatly satisfied the mayor. Still, he wanted more support from the others attending. "Call me, *Warren,*" he replied extending his trademark hook. "I still think you'd make a great one," he said with a wink in his eye. The fast operating mind of Warren Striker was busy at work. In practically the same breath, he pointed at Charles Bentley and pitched his voice. "*You* are one of the reasons why we're sitting here today."

The proud veteran sat up straight absorbing the compliment. Warren continued to navigated the topic by elaborating about, *That war in Europe we had to fight.* His intense brown eyes became more expressive as he bragged about Charlie's military career and embellished over his own. Soon European countries were mentioned along with specific German villages with Charlie's memory being stirred. With perfect timing Warren pretended to recall that "Peter" was from that area. Looking at him, he asked, "Hey, aren't you from there?"

Peter was in good company with Mary Joy Tanga and Ruth Watson being present. Both women were children during WWII and could relate to what Peter was being subjected to. Mary Joy was born in the Philippians and experienced American prejudice when she became a citizen at a young age. Ruth matched her by simply being an African American woman growing up in that era.

They were both amused but not impressed with the mayor's tactic. They paid attention knowing that Peter Constantine would handle the mockery *just right.*

The man of German descent was ready. "Yes I am," he said. "I grew up in those villages you mentioned."

Warren came back at him like a shark and asked in an interrogating manner, "Were you ever in the military?"

"Yes," said Peter, "and I'm proud of it."

Warren dug deeper. Using a smug tone, he asked, "Where did you fight?"

"In Vietnam," came his response. Silence followed with Charlie finally motioning to hear more. Peter explained that his father was a German soldier and migrated his young family to America shortly after WWII. "Our family always felt indebted to the United States and immigrated here in the 1950s. We were all taught English with my goal being to enlist in the army after high school.

Charlie was impressed and gave a salute to his fellow soldier. Peter saluted back with Warren being overshadowed. The ball was now in Peter's court as he immediately switched topics by asking a question that would include everybody. "Does anyone here wish to express any concerns they might have about our town?"

It took no time at all for sixty-five-year-old Grace Collins to voice a complaint. "We need more jobs around here!" she cried out.

Her comment was obviously addressed to Mayor Striker as he squirmed momentarily gathering his composure. "We're setting the stage for that," he said with confidence.

"I only see old buildings being knocked down, but nothing new being built," she said.

"They are just creating the space we need for the new ones," he assured. "Soon we will have more jobs with everyone working again." Skeptical eyes rolled as coffee was being sipped.

Peter came to Warren's aid. "The entire country is in a recession with the economy starting to rebound. We will be well-prepared when that happens with cleared land waiting for new construction." Peter's injection gave a ray of hope with his comment being digested.

"That's right," said Mayor Warren Striker. "We are employing as many as possible to get rid of our obsolete structures in order to upscale local industry when the economy moves forward."

An encouraging thought for those yet to experience the country's economic pattern of a swinging pendulum. This ambiguous scale measures every high tide without promising it would equal the one before. One couldn't help but wonder: if the economy did bounce back; how much ground would it cover? Might it regain what was once lost and revive anything that still had a faint pulse? There were also those that seemed forgotten. Would it be able to penetrate the furthest, most desolate corners of town and perhaps even save the Meadowdale Community Center?

CHAPTER IV

The following morning had drizzle falling from the skies. Julia Mansfield's windshield wipers kept a rhythmic pace with the mist as bright orange caution signs came into view. The signs forewarned about a detour that required traffic to slow down and change lanes. Strategically, they could view the entire revision with fluorescent cones channeling the road down to one lane. It was all a self-explanatory configuration further assisted by a flag person directing traffic with a hand-held stop sign.

The delay was a familiar one with the county taking aim at another dilapidated structure.

Chase and his mother slowly approached the woman in reflective safety gear and stopped within ten feet. She appeared middle-aged and wore state-issued safety gear that matched what Chase wore when he sorted recyclable material. The boy waved at the woman who commandeered the traffic, prompting her to smile and give a slight wave back. This caused Chase to lean forward, waving more frantically.

Vehicles from the on-coming lane began to crawl past in single file with Chase taking inventory. Three cars, a school bus and finally an old farmer driving a tractor passed, clearing the reversible one-way lane. The friendly woman began to talk on the radio she was holding. Placing it in her pocket, she turned her sign around where it read "slow". Next she motioned Julia to proceed down the designated path as she waved "bye-bye" to Chase. With excitement, he waved "good-bye" to her as they rolled forward.

Just ahead on their right was a congestion of crews and heavy equipment working in unison. Closest was a white utility truck with county emblems on the door. Its back supported a boom that extended like a firetruck's ladder. It had a large bucket attached on the end that held two men. They were way-up-high on top of a telephone pole defusing old lines that had to come down. Yellow caution tape isolated the work site with the sounds of diesel motors rumbling in the background.

This was the county's ever-consuming demolition crew devouring more territory. Hydraulic monsters worked together in a human-like fashion, allowing the rerouted traffic to view the destruction. A backhoe belched black smoke from its massive engine commanding more power. Its shovel had Gothic iron teeth that swooped down in a barbaric mode. Mercilessly, it toppled the roof that stood before it.

From the opposite side came an equally destructive force. A bulldozer easily plowed through the wooden boards that were once a family's home. In moments, all was reduced to ruins. Within days, only a vacant lot strewn with sawdust would remain.

This was what became of Willow Road, an old thoroughfare that led to a once famous retirement home. A place that deteriorated through the years and eventually became the MCC.

Julia and Chase passed the demolition crew with their path being cleared of all obstructions. Almost immediately, they arrived at the community center and entered the parking lot. Pulling up in front of the main building was a jumbo-size motor home. It was painted with lively colors of red, black and gold that swirled in a modern art fashion. From the side of this bus was a handicap platform lowering a gray-haired man in a wheelchair. Julia parked her car behind the bus.

"Mom, do you know who that is?" asked Chase as he pointed.

"No, I don't, son," she answered. "It must be somebody new that wants to join us today." Chase look at his mother with enthusiasm. He always welcomed anyone who was new to the MCC.

"Mom," he continued. "Is it okay if I feed Humphrey before class starts?"

"Why, of course," she said. "But you have to make it quick. We're running a bit late this morning because of the traffic delay."

"Okay, mom," he responded. "I won't be long and then I'll meet you inside."

"That sounds good, son," she said kissing Chase on the cheek. Chase already had his raincoat on with peanuts in hand. The teen unfastened his seat belt, left the car and ran towards the path that led to the squirrel's home.

Once through the trail, he walked up to the abandoned portable and peered through the glass casing that enclosed the electric meter. To his delight the tiny disk was still turning at a slow speed, giving sign that his friend still lived there. Chase remembered that there was little time to spare and dropped one peanut down the hole that channeled under the old school room. He glanced at the light blue water bowl and saw that it was overflowing from the rain. He sprinkled the remaining nuts around the immediate area. With Humphrey fed, Chase turned around and made a mad dash to his homeroom arriving out of breath.

Chase scanned the room with those present giving a friendly wave. This made the popular boy smile and wave back. Looking around, he saw Ella Ray's traditional 'peace sign' directed towards him. Chase nodded back. A warm 'thumbs up' came by way of Lois Sexton with Chase sending one back. Next he went to the coat rack, draped his wet garment on a hook and took the nearest available seat.

The hungry boy looked over at the desert table. As always it was full of various treats, illustrating the many friends present. The room also had an additional treat: the handicapped man he saw earlier was in their circle.

All eyes turned to the front desk with Chase's mom playing teacher. She politely began class by introducing the man who arrived in the luxurious motor home. "Before we get started, I'd like to introduce a special guest we have with us today," announced Julia.

Sitting next to Renée was the featured guest. The fifty-six-year-old with thinning gray hair rolled out in a dramatic fashion spinning 360 degrees with his right hand extended high for all to see. "Hello everyone," he said in a loud voice. "My name is Andy Rutledge. I have heard many wonderful things about this place and couldn't wait to come here and meet everyone." Andy's charm won everybody over.

"Hi, Andy," cried out different voices throughout the room.

"Hello, everyone!" came his cheerful response.

"Andy has a special treat for everyone," said Renée Klause as her dog barked wagging its tail. All eyes were on him as he blushed. Finally, he spoke up. "I have done artwork my entire life and I'm well aware of the fine work the Meadowdale Community Center is known for. I dropped by to see if I could help out in any way and even learn something." Everyone looked at one-another nodding with approval.

"I am pleased to be here and will spend time getting to know everyone today," said Andy. He then rolled backwards to where he originally was.

"We are glad you could join us today, Andy," said Julie.

Standing up she took command of the room. "But first," she said looking at everyone. Without warning, she threw up confetti with both hands proclaiming, "It's social time!"

"Yea," cheered the whole room. Andy was amused watching. The newcomer jumped right in by using both index fingers to blow a shrill whistle.

Chase was in true form and approached Andy. "This is the time when we get treats and visit with everyone," he explained. "Would you like me to push you to the desert table?"

Andy was the furthest thing from being an invalid. He was also understanding and knew what this honor would mean to Chase. "I'd love that," he said extending his hand. "My name is, *Andy.*"

"My name is, *Chase,*" he replied as they shook hands. Andy rolled forward, positioning the back of the wheelchair towards his new friend. He placed his hands on his lap allowing the boy to push him to the dessert table. Julia watched from a distance with a tear trickling down her face.

Those present showed hospitality by clearing a path for their guest to be first in line. Chase pushed Andy to the end of the table where he reached for a paper plate, cup, plastic utensils and a few napkins. Andy began to fill his plate with Chase advancing him through the buffet with perfect timing. Upon leaving the table, Andy saw Renée motion for him to join her circle. "Thank you very much, Chase," said Andy. "I can take over from here."

"You're welcome, Andy," said Chase. The boy let go of the handles and went to the back of the dessert line. Andy rested the food on his lap and wheeled next to Renée

The social was working according to design. Andy was now getting to know others at a more in-depth level with a smile on his face serving as testimony! Eventually, he found himself next to Justin and commented on how they had wheelchairs from the same manufacturer. A brief conversation took place between the two with Andy asking, "How do you like your chair." He was pleased that Justin was very happy with it and had lots to say.

An hour later the desert social ended with everything having been cleaned up. Julia was once again leading the class and declared the rest of the rainy day 'art day.' At once, the room stood up and formed a single line by the door. Andy followed suit and wheeled himself in line. Next, Julia led the class out of the room and down the hall to the art room. This was a large room with long workbenches, stools and cabinets full of supplies. There were also barrels that had a wide variety of material ranging from colorful plexiglass; to shiny pipes and polished wood. Andy was impressed from what he saw and wanted to work with Chase. He rolled up to the boy's station and asked, "Can I work with you today?"

Chase's eyes lit up. Andy, choose *him* to spend the day with! "Sure," he exclaimed. "I'd like that a lot!" The boy began to explain to him about the recyclable material that they sort through and how some of it was used for art projects. Andy was impressed with how resourceful the MCC was. Chase displayed the project he was working on. It was a wall hanging consisting of fall leaves, pebbles and personalized hand prints mixed in a beautiful colleague. It was framed with wrinkled foil that came from an old heating unit. "This is for my mother," he said with pride.

Andy picked up the picture with both hands and studied it. He had a degree in art and knew talent when he saw it. His face lost all expression as he turned to look at Chase Mansfield. "This is pretty good," he commented in a serious tone.

"Thank you," said the mentally challenged teen.

"I have an idea, Chase," said Andy.

"What?" asked the boy.

"We should have a day at the beach when the weather gets better," suggested the man. "The seashore has many interesting things people use to make great artwork."

"Really?" responded the boy

"Why, sure," he replied in a comforting tone. "Seashells, driftwood, polished rocks and things from ships, boats and even other countries wash up to shore all the time. It's just like what you find here," he explained. "It's all different and every time I go there I see something new."

"Wow!" commented Chase. "That would be neat! We can even spend the day there and have a picnic!"

"We can make a field trip out of it and invite everybody," said Andy. The man in the wheelchair spent the rest of the day with

Chase including lunch time. Together, they stayed as a team and finished the beautiful picture.

Andy couldn't help but marvel at how gifted his new friend was. He kept looking back and forth between the picture and Chase's innocent face. At that moment, the reciprocate of this 'labor of love' entered the room.

The proud son was handed the masterpiece and walked towards his mother saying, "I made this for you, Mom." He gave it to her knowing how happy it would make her.

Julia held it up with both hands and studied it. The mother started to shake with emotion, knowing how hard her son worked on the picture and how much he loved her. She placed the present on a table that was next to her and hugged her son saying, "That's so beautiful! Thanks, Chase. I love you too."

Andy watched in silence with tears running down his face.

Twenty minutes later everyone was outside leaving for home. The mammoth luxury bus with the wheelchair access pulled up where Andy was waiting. He waved at Chase and his mother saying, "It was fun today, and I'll see you two tomorrow. Bye!"

"Bye, Andy," said Chase as he waved back.

"Bye, Andy," said Julia. "It was so nice to meet you. We'll look forward to seeing you tomorrow."

The driver of the bus assisted Andy on the platform. Once secured he was elevated to an open door and rolled himself into the vehicle. The ramp then folded in sections and tucked itself away for traveling. Soon Andy was sitting next to the driver with both men waving at the mother and son team. Chase and his mother waved back as the motor home drove off.

There was much about the friendly man in the wheelchair that was unknown: *Was he married? Does he have a family? And where did he come from?* What was comforting was that he would be back the next day.

Reaching into his pocket Chase discovered that he had a peanut and pulled it out. "Mom," he said in a concerned voice. "I forgot to give Humphrey this peanut. Can I give it to him before we go?"

"Why sure you can," she said. "I'll be waiting in the car."

"Thanks, mom," he replied. The boy raced to the trail with peanut in hand. When he approached the clearing something was wrong.

A strip of yellow caution tape was chest-high, blocking the pasture where Humphrey lived. Looking beyond he saw the *kiss of death:* red paint was sprayed in a continuous squiggly line that wrapped around the old portable. More yellow tape blocked the steps leading to the door. The boy was devastated and stepped under the tape. Standing tall he slowly walked up to the condemned structure and glanced at the electric meter. Looking inside, he noticed that the tiny disc was no longer turning. Fear had overcome him causing his jaw to drop. He took a few steps backwards verifying what stood before him.

Instinctively he tossed the nut near the water bowl, turned and ran for his mother's protection.

CHAPTER V

C hase Mansfield ran to the parking lot and saw his mother waiting with the car running. The boy was confused and in a state of panic. He wondered if he did something wrong and was being punished. He entered the vehicle, closed the door and fastened his seat belt.

Julia put the car in gear and began the drive home. The ride was peaceful with the windshield wipers keeping pace with the constant tapping of rain. "I love that picture you made for me," she said. The boy was preoccupied in thought and acknowledged her with a slight motion. "Is anything wrong, Chase?" she asked.

"I just want to go home," he answered. Julia sensed that something was troubling her son. She honored his privacy by allowing the boy to discuss it on his terms. The remainder of the drive was quiet with the defroster's constant sound giving a soothing tranquilizing affect.

Chase's quiet mode continued at the dinner table with his uncle John having already been tipped off. John Mansfield was Julia's older brother and lived with them. In essence; he was Chase's father figure. He was handsome with fine brown hair and eyes that matched his sisters. Distinct facial features with a mustache further carried his Mansfield traits. He was a middle-aged man of average height and weight. The three were definitely a happy family with John filling the void of Chase's absent father. A man the boy never knew.

As dinner completed, Chase began to open up. "Uncle John," he asked. "Can I ask you something?"

Julia gave a slight smile at her loving brother as he responded. "Of course you can," he replied.

"After dinner can we go outside so that I can show you something?" asked the boy.

The first piece of the puzzle was about to present itself. "That would be great," said John.

For the first time that evening, Chase seemed a little relaxed and ventured into his dessert. John looked over to his sister with her discretely giving a 'thumbs up.'

When dinner was over Julia said, "I'll stay here and put everything away." This allowed John to immediately address what was concerning his nephew. "Let's go outside now," he said to the boy. "You can show me what you're talking about."

"Okay," agreed Chase. They got up and went to the living room closet. Rain gear was donned, with John grabbing an umbrella. They left the house with Chase leading. John was led to the side of the house with Chase pointing at an electric meter that was enclosed in a glass bubble. "What's that?" he asked. The uncle stood next to him sharing the umbrella.

"Oh, that thing," replied John. "That's a meter that shows the power company how much electricity we are using."

Chase knew about electricity. He remembered the time when a power outage shut down the television, lights and heat. He had another question. Pointing at the meter, he asked, "What do those numbers mean?"

"Those numbers identify who lives here," said John.

The wheels were turning in Chase's head as he grasped the concept. "Like the numbers on our house the mailman uses to bring us our mail?" he questioned.

"Right," replied John.

Chase digested the information. It was obvious that his questions were answered with John saying, "Let's get inside now."

At bedtime, Chase and his mother were closing their nightly visit after saying their goodnight prayers. "Mom," asked the boy.

"What is it, son," she answered.

"Do you love Humphrey?" he asked.

Laughingly she said, "Of course I do; everybody does."

"If Humphrey lost his home, what would happen?" he asked.

"Then we would just have to find him another home, that's all." Julia leaned over and hugged her son. She kissed him on the cheek saying, "I love you, Chase. Good night."

The boy was feeling more comfortable and said, "I love you too, Mom. Good night." The mother tucked her son in bed. Leaving the room, she turned off the light and shut the door.

The next morning Chase and his mother were driving to the community center. They passed a graded lot where a condemned small house stood the previous day. The ever-present demolition crew had claimed their most recent victim and was now resting on the edge of the MCC. Chase saw the whole picture and had knots in his stomach. The mother and son entered the parking lot with a luxury bus passing them in the opposite direction. Chase felt a little better knowing that his new friend would be close at hand.

At that moment, the loud growling of heavy equipment followed the crunching sound of dried wood. Chase was fully aware of what was happening. He also knew that he was restricted to enter the area where the demolition crew was working. Worried about Humphrey's safety, he said a prayer. Through his faith, he found the courage needed to survive the day and went to his homeroom.

The morning routine at the MCC followed as usual with Steve Smith heading the class. After social hour, the day was dedicated to rummaging through recyclable material that awaited on their loading dock. Once the chore was finished, art class would follow.

Soon they were at the loading dock with Steve having situated everything. Andy had already visited with Chase that morning and seemed to be working with Steve and his son, Allen that day. Chase and his fellow classmates inspected the three pallets that were delivered recently. The scene was like an art gallery, with everyone viewing at a different angle.

At that moment, something peculiar caught Chase's attention. The electric meter from Humphrey's abandoned portable was spotted and appeared to be looking directly at him. It was definitely the very one that marked his friend's home with the positioning of distinct capital letters making it unmistakable. The small round meters inside the glass casing resembled lonesome eyes begging for a home. The tiny disc protruded a smile of hope.

As Chase walked around the congestion, the Martian-type face seemed to follow him like a sunflower plant guided by light.

Chase wasted no time. He took the meter and placed it into his personal supply bucket.

The fifteen-year-old looked up with a spiritual gratitude. He was always God-fearing and within his heart, *knew* this was *meant* to be. Next he picked items that seemed complimentary to his find. Rusted conduit, metal lamp shades from old streetlights, and fragments from electrical units were placed in his bucket.

Within a half-hour, all desirable scraps were taken with the remainder allocated to its proper recycle bins. Art class would be the next stop. Chase Mansfield carried his scrap bucket to the class and placed it on his assigned work bench. His mind was fast at work knowing he could acquire enough material to make a feeder for Humphrey.

Equally important, he would find him a new home using the numbers inside the electric meter to guide him there. The boy went through the obsolete metal and saw two vintage street-lamp shades of different sizes. From there, he pulled out three rusted electrical pipes that measured the same.

Without hesitation, he walked up to Steve and asked for help. "That's why I'm here," he said in a friendly manner. They went to Chase's table with the boy explaining what he wanted. Andy was nearby and rolled his wheelchair to watch while being undetected. Chase positioned the pipes on the table like a teepee and asked if he could weld the pipes together. He also wanted the lamp shades being fastened inside the metal poles. This idea would have the larger shade welded on the lower level with the rods securing the smaller one on a higher level. "What is it going to be?" asked Steve.

"A feeder for Humphrey," replied the student. Steve knew of the beloved squirrel and realized that the shades were meant to be up-side-down to serve as bowls.

"I'll take care of that right now, boss," said Steve. He grabbed the pipes, lamp shades and walked to the enclosed welding area. Chase could see sparks fly above the fireproof curtain with a popping sound as Steve welded the pieces together.

In a few minutes, Steve returned wearing his welding helmet with the face shield raised above his forehead. "Is this what you want?" he asked placing the tripod on his bench. It was lined-up perfect with all three sides being equidistant and sturdy. "Can you do one more thing for me?" asked Chase.

"Anything for you," replied Steve.

Chase took the electric meter out of the bucket and held it just above the metal frame. "Can you put this right here?" he asked.

Steve opened his hand with Chase giving him the meter. He took it along with the metal stand and went back to the welding area. A few pops and sparks later he returned and set Chase's design on the table facing him. The boy was taken with the alien-like structure staring back. A huge grin came across his face. Behind the boy sat Andy at a loss for words. For the second time that week he witnessed Chase's artistic genius.

The first Meadowdale Feeder was born with Chase Mansfield being a proud papa!

CHAPTER VI

W arren Striker spent the past few days dwelling over his recent visit at the veteran's hall. Full of stress and anxiety he spent the past mornings soul searching. He knew he put his foot in his mouth trying to upstage Peter Constantine. He also struck out when Grace Collins attacked him with her comment about, *"The town needing more jobs."* A constant remark he hears almost every day. Each time his political opponent handled the situation with class, winning everybody over.

Time was making the situation worse. He was elected based on a campaign promise to get everyone back to work. A situation that never improved since he took office. Warren paced back and forth with his head lowered. *"There must be something I can do to change things around here,"* he thought to himself...

His thoughts were interrupted by his nephew, Paul calling out to him through an intercom. "Uncle Warren, you wanted a thirty minute reminder before your meeting with the police department."

Warren leaned over the intercom on his desk and pushed the 'talk' button. "Thanks, Paul; I'll be out the rest of the day."

"Okay, Uncle Warren," came an immediate response.

The Mayor was punctual as always arriving at the Meadowdale Police Station on time. The morning visit consisted of coffee, two boxes of donuts, ten police officers, one sheriff and an incumbent that could make others laugh on demand. Handshakes along with compliments and promises closed off the event with repeat performances to be given at the fire department and Lion's Club.

31

His cheerful smile found time to drop by The Meadowdale Review and share his last box of donuts. Often such visits stimulated a slow news day with the mayor's picture hitting the press. The day was dedicated for campaigning, causing the muscles in Mayor Striker's face to get sore. It was now time for Warren to take off his game face, drive home and be himself...

Warren Striker's life was one of day and night. During the day he was a dynamic individual with humor, wit and charm. A 'people person' that made you feel important in his company. That guy you felt you knew your entire life.

Night time was a different story. The man lived alone and had never married. In fact, outside of politics he seldom did anything with anyone. He lived in a modest white house off of a country road that always had an American flag waving from the front porch. Inside were pictures of his political career with high school annuals on the coffee table. His mother, father, sister and brother held a spot near the fireplace.

This was the *real* Warren Striker. A lonely man that nobody knew after hours.

He entered his home and went straight to the kitchen with his evening routine underway. Masterfully, he coordinated his hook and hand by taking an iron skillet from a cabinet, placing it on a burner and turning on the heating unit. Next he opened the refrigerator and removed a plate with a steak on it. Placing it in the skillet, he set the plate next to the stove and reached above for some seasoning.

Soon the sizzling sound of a steak being fried could he heard with smoke rising. Warren used a fork and turned the steak over adding the seasoning. He kept an eye on it, occasionally flipping it. Using a steak knife, he cut into the side and verified it was cooked medium well. Turning off the burner, he flipped the meat a final time, grabbed a folded dish towel and wrapped it around the hot skillet handle. He picked it up and slid the hot meal on the plate next to the stove.

Using the knife, he cut several bite-size pieces and skewered them with his hook. Warren walked to his back deck and sat on the steps with his shoes resting on the lawn. In a singing voice, he called out. "Maxwell, Maxwell. Come here, kitty." Affectionately he whistled and made kissing sounds.

A slinky figure crawled out from a bush responding to his call. "Meow," cried out a black and white cat with pasty fur.

The feline seemed to bend as it limped forward, stopping at a safe distance. Sitting upright the stray patiently waited to be fed. Warren wanted to break the barrier and have the animal allow him to pick it up and pet it. The cat with wild whiskers that resembled bristles from an old broom stayed put in defiance.

Warren leaned as far forward as possible extending the kabob. The cat was all too familiar with this stand-off and only stared back.

"Here, kitty, kitty," sang out Warren as he made more kissing sounds. "Maxwell, Maxwell," he called out. The meal was getting cold with Warren finally surrendering. He took the pieces off of his hook, and one-by-one, gently tossed them towards the wild animal. Maxwell went to the closest piece and devoured it. Soon all three pieces were gone with the transient returning to the bushes and disappearing.

Warren sat on the steps feeling dejected. It seemed that nobody had anything to do with him unless he was handing something out.

———————

The next morning the saga continued. Mayor Warren Striker was in his office looking at the morning's paper his nephew handed him. The front page showed a line of people at the local food bank. It was the featured story that told of how the town of Meadowdale had been deteriorating economically in recent years. Various citizens were interviewed with certain comments printed:

"I lost my home."

"Whose going to help us?"

"Some of my neighbors had to move away to start all over."

This outcry was inadvertently directed to the town's leadership with non-other than Mayor Warren Striker on top of the pyramid. It was a disgrace.

There was more.

Below the article was a picture of volunteers serving the increasing numbers at a local bread line. One of which was a bald man with an eye patch dipping a ladle into a large pot of soup. Warren's knuckles turned white as he shook the paper. This was one of many press releases that inauspiciously promoted his rival.

Thumbing towards the back of the paper, he saw a small picture of his cheesy grin swinging his trademark hook. The article was 'filler' just above an advertisement for a local tire shop. It highlighted his recent visit to the 'Review' stating on how his charm touched those who were present.

Warren Striker was a fighter and would not take this lying down. He was also smart and knew *how to win.* He would simply call his new *friend* and schedule an informal get-together. A ploy to study his opponent on a more personal level.

Warren put the paper down and pulled his cell phone out of his pocket. Looking at the local phone directory, he found Peter's phone number and took the fight to him. The Mayor winked at his nephew as Peter answered his phone.

"Is that any way to address a friend?" he barked out in a jovial manner.

There was a pause with Warren listening to Peter's response. Immediately he volleyed back with his quick wit. "Hey, that's my line, Mayor Constantine!" Laughter traveled through the receiver with Warren controlling the conversation. "That's a good idea," he continued. "Does tomorrow work for you?" At that moment, the mayor opened a drawer and pulled out a pen with a note pad. "Are you ready?" he asked. Warren recited his home address along with his phone number. Next, he wrote down Peter's.

34

"Saturday sounds good," replied Warren. There was a final pause with the closing words being exchanged. "I feel the same and always feel free to drop by whenever you feel like it... Okay... See you this Saturday." With a satisfied look, he ended the call and placed his phone on the desk. Leaning back in his chair, he folded his arms and addressed his nephew. "And now we'll find out what we need to know about our competition," he said with a Cheshire grin on his face.

Paul Blades looked back at his uncle in admiration.

CHAPTER VII

C hase Mansfield held an artist's paintbrush with his right hand. "Good, Chase," said his friend, Andy. "Now stay relax and dab just the tip of the brush into the paint..."

Chase was being mentored by Andy Rutledge and followed his instructions. "Now remember to twist the brush as you slide it over the edge of the paint can, just as you did before." The student laid the bristles covered with yellow/green paint where Andy suggested and in one motion, turned his wrist as he pulled it away. "Excellent, Chase. Now apply it on the frame in the same fashion," reminded the man in the wheelchair. Chase did exactly that. He lay the brush sideways on the metal stand of the feeder and turned it slightly, removing it at once. Another imprint resembling a leaf with fall colors was applied to the stand that held the defunct electric meter.

"Let's stand back and see what we've done so far," suggested Andy as he rolled back. Chase laid the brush on the newspaper that the project rested on and got up to join Andy. What they saw was the result of several day's work. The meter was covered with newspaper taped in place. This prevented any paint from accidentally getting on it.

When Steve Smith asked earlier if he wanted to do more to the feeder; Chase had an immediate answer. "Yes, I want to paint it."

Steve said, "Andy is the man you want to see."

Chase confronted Andy and asked him if he could help him paint the feeder he was working on. "Me?" questioned the man in a surprised tone. "I'd be honored! Do you have any ideas on how you want to paint it?" he asked.

"I want it to look like it is outside and have it the same color that the leaves are," said Chase. With that request made, Andy took the boy under his wing and shared his expertise in painting.

What was once a discolored metal frame with makeshift bowls was now a forest green pedestal with red, orange and yellow/green leaf patterns. A monument that would draw attention to the numbers needed to guide Humphrey home. "We'll let it dry tonight and put enamel over it tomorrow," said Andy. "By the way, did you give it a name yet?"

Chase looked at his creation and said, "I want to name it, *Sparkles*.

That night at dinner Julia had a surprise for Chase. Steve and his son, Allen were invited over as guests. This made the evening a festive occasion with Steve and John being close friends. It was an informal self-serve meal with spaghetti, salad and soft drinks accompanied with humorous stories. Tales rotated around the table with side-splitting laughter causing periodical time-outs. Finally, Allen addressed the much talked about feeder Chase made at the MCC.

John was all ears being the only one present that hadn't seen it yet. "Tell me about it Chase," said his uncle. "I've heard so much talk about it."

Chase sat up straight and began to describe the futuristic *squirrel feeder* he designed. The boy went into detail explaining about using the *right* electric meter so that Humphrey could see the numbers to his new home (once Chase found one for him).

The brother and sister were hit hard by that piece of information. They remembered the evening when they compared notes about Chase asking about the numbers on the electric meter to their house and about what to do if Humphrey ever lost his home. Julia told John about the county leveling the portable at the community center where the squirrel lived. The *why* behind Chase's masterpiece was now understood.

Julia looked at her brother as he looked back. Tears ran down her face as she abruptly covered her mouth and left for the bathroom. John had a lump in his throat realizing how much his nephew loved the maimed animal. Steve and Allen knew that the feeder was for the squirrel Chase adopted, but didn't realize that it was part of a plan to get it a new home. Many times all three witnessed Chase feeding the wild pet with the chopped tail and grew attached to it.

"Is mom okay?" asked Chase.

"She's just fine," responded John. "She just needed to use the bathroom, that's all."

There was silence until Steve picked up the ball. "Did you feed Humphrey today?" he asked.

"No," answered a dejected Chase. "I haven't seen him since they took his home away." The boy looked down and started to cry. "I leave nuts for him every morning," he said raising his head. "But I don't see him anymore." Looking at the table, he asked in fear, "Do you think he ran away?"

Allen was quick. "Not at all. He's just found a good hiding place until he gets a new home."

"Allen's right," said Steve. "Humphrey loves you too much to go away."

"Humphrey is just waiting for things to calm down, that's all," said his uncle.

Chase was happy to hear the words of encouragement and calmed down. John, Steve and Allen looked at one-another. Nothing had to be said; they all knew what they were thinking...

———————

The following afternoon while Chase and Andy were applying enamel on the feeder, Steve, Allen and John were outside with their fishing nets. They were on *squirrel patrol* looking to capture Humphrey.

They went to the small clearing where the old portable use to stand. Being the sophisticated beings they were; they huddled and devised a plan. They agreed to place a few peanuts in the center of the lawn and hide at opposite corners; waiting for the unsuspecting rodent to feed. Once it was out in the open, it would find itself surrounded; making its capture a *breeze*. The prisoner would then be placed in an escape-proof wooden cage that John built the previous night. It was the size of a bread box with a removable mesh screen that sealed the top.

Fishing nets were visible above the shrubs where the hunters hid. Patiently they waited for Humphrey. Almost forty minutes passed when John called out, "There he is!"

The pet was in the center of the field placing a peanut in its mouth when all at once, the brigade closed in. It was obvious that the trio hadn't practiced their maneuvers and resembled the Keystone Cops on a butterfly expedition.

Allen was closest and walled off the area where the alarmed squirrel initially tried to run. Humphrey changed directions with Allen's net missing by inches. His second try also missed its mark and clobbered his father in the shin. Steve dropped his net and screamed involuntarily, rolling on the moist ground as he clasped his lower leg with both hands. John's effort also proved futile. He lacked the hand-eye coordination to trap an unorthodox moving object with a peanut in its mouth. The four legged creature vanished in the bushes leaving the score:

Humphrey–1

Humans–0

Tired and exhausted, the threesome would swallow their pride, regroup and try again. With one member icing a welt for weeks to come. It was comforting to know, however, that Chase's friend was alive and well.

The following afternoon gave further testimony to the independence of the local animal community. It was Saturday with Warren Striker sitting on the steps of his back deck. His hook was baited with tantalizing steak cooked and seasoned to perfection. A fresh smile on his face resembled a used car salesman talking to a teenager. The expression coincided with his 'happy as a lark' serenading to the resident feral. Leaning forward, he extended the bribe closer with hopes to lure his subject.

"Maxwell," he sang out. "Come heeerre, Maxwell. Here, kitty, kitty." Pleasant whistling along with kissing sounds were being employed, but to no avail.

The cat seemed bored with his antics and remained put. The meal was getting cold with Warren finally giving in and removing the tasty morsels from his hook. Tossing the meat towards Maxwell, he watched the cat approach each piece and consume it within seconds.

"That cat loves you," came a voice off to the side. Warren was startled and turned around to see Peter Constantine standing at the gate that led to his back yard. This jarred his memory, remembering that earlier in the week they agreed to get together that day. He also recalled encouraging him to could drop by *whenever he felt like it.* Realizing that his cell phone was left inside the house, Peter's unannounced visit constituted fair play.

Peter looked at Warren with compassion. From the moment they met, he detected pain within the man. A pain that was well hidden, making the political leader appear less vulnerable. "What's your friend's name?" he asked.

"Maxwell," replied Warren. He was sensitive about having the most precious moment of his day intruded upon and became defensive. "It it wrong to love a needy animal?" he asked.

Peter tipped the scales even. "Not at all," he said. "Maxwell reminds me of Karl."

"Who's Karl?" asked Warren with a contorted face.

"Meet me in my car and I'll show you," said Peter.

It took no time for Warren Striker to answer. "I'll be there in five minutes."

Soon they were driving to the other side of town where Peter Constantine lived. Pulling up in the driveway Warren was pleasantly surprised to see that Peter's house was a modest rambler. It was also the only home in the neighborhood with the nation's flag waving. Peter led Warren to his back yard and saw that it opened up to an undeveloped field. Peter also had a wood deck just off the ground. He stepped up on the deck and opened what appeared to be an old milk box. Reaching inside he pulled out a plastic bag full of bread crumbs.

Walking onto the lawn, he projected his voice towards a cluster of trees. "Karl," he called out. "Feeding time, Karl." At once a swarm of sparrows flew from the trees and towards them. Reaching in the bag, he grabbed some bread crumbs and threw a small handful off to his far right. The sparrows dived for it. Warren didn't understand and asked, "Which one is Karl?"

"There he is," pointed Peter. Behind the flock was a bird that lagged behind. It appeared to be smaller than the others and had a noticeable bent feather. Warren's chest puffed out seeing the injustice. "This is our only chance to feed him, but we must be quick," said Peter in a hurried voice. Opening the bag Warren grabbed a handful of crumbs with Peter getting more. Running out to the field both men cried out, "Karl. Here, Karl..." They intercepted the crippled sparrow and threw the bread crumbs in front of it. Karl quickly landed and was able to eat two pieces before the rest of the flock came and took the rest.

In victory, the men jumped up and down with Warren yelling, "Atta boy, Karl!"

Warren saw the smile on Peter's face with a tear running down his lone eye. Peter slowly turned to Warren realizing what he just exposed about himself. An understanding was established with the realization they have both had been hurt in life. Peter opened up more by saying, "So, you know what it's like to always be the last one picked on the playground."

A teary-eyed Warren Striker replied, "If you even got picked, you did better than me."

The conversation took a turn with Warren wanting to extend his time with Peter. "Hey," he said. "Weren't we suppose to do something today? I can fire up my barbeque and get some steaks going."

Peter had something to say. "Warren, you and I are bachelors that spend every night at home. This is Saturday; let's go out and be guys. We can get a pizza somewhere and visit."

Warren thought about it and realized that getting out would be good medicine. "I couldn't agree with you more!" he exclaimed.

It was just getting dark when a 'Benard's Special' with extra cheese was delivered to their table. Benard's was a popular pizzeria in the heart of town. Neither man had his guard up with humorous confessions trading back and forth.

Peter reeled off a story about his teenage years trying to impress girls. He pointed out that with his accent, receding hairline and a glass eye that was never adjusted right made him a 'professional clown.' Peter was almost hyperventilating when he commented, "At least everyone in school knew who I was."

"That's pretty big of you to admit that to a guy that's trying to beat you in an election," laughed Warren with both hands pressed against his stomach. "But, I do think I have you covered on this one." Grabbing another slice of pizza, Warren took a big bite and gathered his thoughts.

"I'm all ears," chimed Peter as he took a drink of coke.

"Do you remember what an Edsel was?" he asked.

"Of course," answered Peter.

"Good," replied Warren. "My first car was a 1959 Edsel that my uncle encouraged me to buy. He told me that they were going to be classics soon with women lining up to be with anyone who had one." Both men began to chuckle remembering the embarrassing flop the car proved to be. Warren took a drink and continued. "Soooo, I bought one that was for sale before anyone else could jump my claim."

Peter was giggling and wanted to hear more.

Warren was a new man that night. He was able to listen to someone without having to be *better than them.* He could also laugh at himself without scaring his pride. The short man with a complex went into great detail about how unpopular he was in high school. He even elaborated on how he got caught up with the fashions of the 1970s as an attempt to fit in.

"Do you remember those short, fat guys in high school that wore the platform shoes?" he asked.

By this time, Peter was leaning to one side as he broke out into hysterics. "You mean the ones with the floppy hats?" he remarked.

"Hey!" exclaimed Warren pointing back. "I still have mine." Peter almost fell out of the booth. Warren went on to paint a graphic picture on how ridiculous he looked in his trendy outfit driving the ultimate nightmare from the auto industry. "My personality needed some work too," he added.

"And where is that car now?" asked Peter.

"Where I left it," said Warren. "When it dawned on me what a fool it made out of me; I parked it next to my parent's house and it's been there ever since."

Peter knew that Warren was homegrown and realized that the car had to be somewhere nearby. The evening winded down with Peter seeing the bill first and buying. That was another plus for the day. In such situations, Warren would usually buy to flex his muscle. He didn't mind playing 'second fiddle' and left the tip.

Soon Warren was being dropped off at his home with Peter thanking him for a great day. "I had a great time too!" said Warren as he got out of the car. "Next time it's on me, Peter."

"Ya got a deal," he replied. Warren closed the door with Peter tapping the horn and driving off. Once inside his home, Warren felt *right.* For the first time in his entire life, he went out on a Saturday night with a *friend.*

CHAPTER VIII

C hase Mansfield left church with his mother and uncle. It was Sunday with the weekly tradition of going out for pancakes just ahead. The outing was to discuss Pastor Arnold's sermon and dedicate their week to apply the lesson it taught. This was definitely 'quality time,' with hot syrup poured over a stack of buttermilk pancakes making it fun!

Several bites into the meal, Chase pointed out that the pastor talked about caring for others, no matter *who* they were. "Does that include, Humphrey?" he asked.

Julia and John looked at each other and smiled at Chase's innocence. She glanced at the boy saying, "Yes it does."

John spoke next and elaborated about how caring for others always made his life happier. "It even makes me look forward to going to work," he said.

Julia was next and mentioned on how the MCC made her happy because it was all about caring for others.

Chase had been preoccupied over the missing squirrel and continued talk about it. Finally after several rounds he asked, "Can we go to the community center after breakfast and look for him?"

Julia looked at her brother with him giving a nod of approval. Looking at her son she said, "That would be wonderful."

Chase had an ear to ear grin as he poured more syrup over the hotcakes.

Once the car was parked at the community center, Chase got out and ran to the trail that led to Humphrey's stomping grounds. The caretaker was already prepared, having a few peanuts in his pocket. He reached the clearing where the old portable once stood. It was now a smooth dirt patch with no signs of an electric meter ever standing there.

A new water bowl was put into service days ago when Chase noticed the old blue one was gone. He placed the white bowl where the last one rested, throwing a peanut near it. The boy winced as he yelled out in all directions. "Humphrey, Humphrey..." Frantically he reached into his pocket and grabbed more nuts. Throwing them where a hole once burrowed into the ground, he continued to call out. "Humphrey, Humphrey..."

It was painful for Julia and John to watch. Projecting her voice, she said, "He's probably visiting some of his friends."

John assisted. "He's just like you, Chase; Humphrey has lots of friends."

Chase was out of peanuts. He heard what his mother and uncle said and began to calm down. At that moment, an idea crossed his mind that gave him hope. "Do you think he went to the animal shelter to visit his friends?" he asked.

Julia knew where this was going. Immediately her brother gently elbowed her giving a sign of approval. "He has probably been there many times," she said in a motherly tone. "But we can drop by and see if he's still visiting." Chase wasted no time and ran to the car hoping to cross paths with his pet.

The Meadowdale Animal Shelter was another underfunded project down the road. What was once a thriving dairy farm was now a makeshift shelter for strays and abandoned pets. Faded tones of red paint covered the vintage structure that resembled the MCC. It was the love of volunteers and private donations that kept its heart beating.

Soon the family was in the parking lot with a pleasant finding. A white van with a wheelchair access was parked by the front door.

The vehicle curtains displayed repetitious patterns of crosses on Mount Calvary requiring no introduction. Maria Rodriguez was spending part of her Sunday doing volunteer work. This meant that her son, Justin would undoubtedly be with her. A friend from the MCC who partook in many sleepovers and trips to the movie theater. Not quite a lost squirrel with a bobbed tail, but a good consolation.

The Mansfields entered the animal shelter with Maria sitting at the front desk. Immediately she ran up to Julia and embraced her. "It's so nice to see you," she said.

"It's always good to see you, too," exclaimed Julia.

"Let me in on this," said John as he wrapped his arms around both women.

The boy in the wheelchair was just down the hall and heard the voices. He turned around and saw a lanky posture with curly blonde hair staring back. A smile came across his face as he wheeled forward saying, "Good morning, *amigo.*"

The classmate from South America was a special friend. Not only did they attend the MCC together, but they also did a variety of things after school. In fact, Justin noticed Chase's interest in his culture and occasionally taught him tidbits from his native tongue.

"Good morning, *amigo,*" answered Chase.

Chase was happy to see his friend knowing he would help. "Do you know if Humphrey is here?" he asked with sincere eyes.

Justin and his mother knew of the deformed squirrel that Chase loved so much. Naturally, they assumed that he wondered if it was housed with the other animals. "I haven't noticed him, but we can look," replied Justin.

"Okay," said Chase. Justin spun around and led Chase down the hall where the unclaimed pets were shelved. Their mere presence activated a whirlwind of barks and meows emulating a chanting distress signal. It echoed in a synchronized rhythm that included wagging tails and outstretched paws of hope. Walking down the corridor, the cries for help increased. In desperation, shiny black noses pressed against the metal screens that confined them.

The boys entered the area where the hallway divided the incarcerated residents. Systematically, they inspected the first cage located on the top-right and progressively covered the entire room in an up-and-down, side-to side sequence.

"Humphrey, are you in there?" called out Chase as he peered into each cage. The compassionate teen could not find his friend but made an important discovery.

Every stop had lonesome eyes staring back with tails standing tall and others wagging. Whiskers rubbed against metal screens with soft coats of fur exposed for petting. The scenario reminded Chase of himself and his many friends at the MCC. *If more people knew of this place, every cage would be empty,* he thought to himself. The cuddly faces begging for a home would always be engrained in his memory. This opened Chase's heart further, giving him more capacity to love and address another good cause. The boy would go on to share a lesson he learned long ago:

Animals have feelings just like people.

After their search Chase went back to the lobby and addressed his mother and uncle. "I guess Humphrey is playing somewhere with his other friends," he casually said.

Chase, Julia and John said their goodbyes to Maria and her son and left.

"See you at the MCC," said Julia in parting.

"Okay, see you there," responded Maria.

Once in the car, Chase asked what happens to the animals that never get to leave. "They stay there and keep each other happy," said John.

Julia made a comment. "Since we're visiting today, we might as well see mom on the way home."

"That's what I was about to say," answered John.

Chase's face lit up. He loved visiting his 'Grandma Becky' and listening to her stories.

"That will be great," he said.

The Meadowdale Retirement Home was a slight improvement compared to the MCC and animal shelter. A standard that at best would be considered *acceptable*. It was a two-story colonial structure painted a traditional white with black trim. A cobblestone road led to the main entrance with a modest courtyard consisting of a few benches, statues, a pond, flower garden and a birdbath. John let Julia and Chase out in front of the main doors and said, "I'll meet you in her room."

"Okay, John," said his sister. The mother and son got out of the car and walked the series of steps that advanced to the main doors. Upon entering the one-hundred-year-old building, a climate change took place. The purity of country-fresh air was replaced with the penetrating smell of an ammonia disinfectant. The abrupt change also carried a distinct faint odor of mold; a familiar introduction that accompanies all senior housing complexes. The 'handshake' that hits everyone's senses with full force.

The ambiance of the retirement home continued. Its decor was a theme of resourcefulness with mismatching furniture, lamps and wall hangings encompassing the entire building. The encouragement of social awareness laced the community with cards, puzzles and board games in plain view. An open invitation for *anyone* to join in. Bookshelves batted clean-up by supplying trade magazines and outdated books for those who had no one.

Julia and Chase walked to the receptionist at the front desk. The gracious woman with wavy shoulder-length silver hair needed no introduction. Her name was Valery Tomkins, a stay-at-home mom who did her job and the pride of the local Rotary Club. The sixty-two-year-old with wire-rimmed glasses was spending her golden years maintaining her course. She was a non-stop contribution to the town in which she was raised. The receptionist noticed Julia and her son the moment they entered the lobby. "Julia," she said, "it's so nice to see you two today."

"It will soon be three once John parks the car," said Julia with a giggle.

"Well, good," said Valery. "Now if we can get everyone else in the world to follow your example." The widow with three sons meant what she said. Her parents were once residences at the home many years ago; an experience that opened her eyes to the many that never had visitors. A cruel reality. Valery could relate to Julia's family. They visited their mother at least a few times a week and often got her out. Julia signed the daily guest book as John entered the room. "Enjoy your visit and tell your mom I say, "Hi," said Valery.

"I promise," replied Julia.

Walking to the stairways that led to room 214, they saw an old man wearing a red baseball cap. The rigid eighty-eight-year-old was sitting and had a cane between his legs with both hands clasped over the top. Addressing Chase he called out in a trembling voice, "I bet you are good at playing checkers." In front of the senior who weighed almost one-hundred pounds was a game of checkers waiting to be played. The chair facing the table was vacant with Chase's name on it.

The mother and uncle saw hope in the lonely man's eyes. They were also aware that Chase loved playing checkers. "Why don't you play a game and make a new friend?" suggested Julia. "You know where your Grandmother Becky's room is, and you can meet us there when you are done playing." That was music to the old-timer's ears with Chase eager to play.

"Gee, thanks, mom!" came his reply.

Unbeknownst to him, Chase Mansfield would once again make a difference. A feat he accomplished on a day-to-day basis. Sitting down at the available chair, the hospitable senior asked, "What's your name?"

"Chase," answered the boy.

"That's a wonderful name," he replied. "My name is, Harvey Connors. How about you moving first?" he offered. Chase was sitting on the side with the red checkers and moved a center piece first. The game was underway with a conversation already initiated. Harvey asked Chase many questions ranging from where he was from; to what interests he had.

Chase held up his end by answering Harvey's questions and showing interest in return. "How long have you lived here?" asked Chase.

"Over thirty years," said Harvey.

"You must like it here," commented Chase.

"It's not bad living here," said Harvey. "It can get mighty lonely though." The man who was almost ninety explained on how aging often means having fewer people in one's life. "There are even those who don't have anybody," he stressed. Chase looked at the man's soulful face and saw his battle to be loved and surrounded by caring people. It was the same expression of hope he saw at the animal shelter.

The old man was sharp and possibly let Chase win a close game. "We need to play another game when you come by again," he said. Chase agreed. He loved playing checkers and more important, loved others.

The boy thanked Harvey for his hospitality and promised to see him every time he visited his grandmother. He left the table and was soon in room 214 hugging his grandma Becky. "I love you so much, Chase!" she said with both arms around him.

Chase had a tear in his eye after listening to Harvey. "I love you too, grandma," he said. The visit continued with laughter and wonderful stories.

When offered to go out for lunch, she explained that she had just eaten and was getting tired. "I'll take a rain check," she said.

Within a half hour, they were home having tuna fish sandwiches and chicken noodle soup. Chase talked about his new friend,

Harvey. "Now I know where to go whenever I want to play checkers," he said.

"We can drop you off there when your mom and I are busy," said John. "This way you'll have plenty of time to play checkers with Harvey and still visit your grandma."

Chase loved the idea! "That would be great," he said. "I bet there are other people there too that would want to play checkers."

It took Julia no time to respond. "There are many living there that would love to spend time with you." The son digested her comment, giving him more to talk about. He began to elaborate on how that morning's visits made him more aware about the pain that came with loneliness. "Harvey was just like the cats and dogs at the animal shelter," he pointed out. "I wish that every person in the whole world would help every cat, dog and old person that was lonely.

"It all starts with caring for one person at a time," said his uncle, John. Chase absorbed what he said. Without any thought his friend, Justin came to mind. "Like Justin?" he asked.

"Yes," said his mother, "like Justin."

Another thought entered Chase's mind. "Can Justine stay the night?" he asked. "We can watch cartoons and go to school together."

"I don't see why not," his mother said. "I'll call Maria after lunch." The meal continued with a huge smile on Chase Mansfield's face. When the last bite was taken, Chase and his uncle cleared the table with Julia making an important phone call. She returned moments later addressing her son. "Does pizza for you and Justin sound good for dinner tonight?" she asked. "You guys can have it while watching your shows."

Chase ran to his mother and hugged her. "Thanks, mom!" he said.

"You have just made someone very happy," she said. "Justin will be in his fold-up wheelchair so he can go to school with us tomorrow."

"That's great," he said. "After dinner I'll push him around our neighborhood. Maybe we'll see Humphrey," he added. That comment hit home with John. He left the room to make *his important call.*

Later that evening Chase and Justin were in the family room enjoying pizza with root beer. Muffled laughter was occasionally heard throughout the house while they watched their favorite cartoon shows. In the dining room, John and his sister were just finishing their meal when a knock came from the front door. Julia was suspicious about John's private phone call earlier and got up first to see who it was. Approaching the entryway she saw John's trout net propped next to the homemade cage. The items lay inauspiciously by the front door waiting to be deployed.

Opening the door, she saw the father and son team of Steve and Allen Smith armed with fishing nets. Stern faces telegraphed that they were there on business. Preoccupied in thought, they quietly acknowledged Julia. John had already entered the room and picked up his trapping utensils. Looking at his sister he gave a 'thumbs-up' before going out on their *secret mission.* She returned fire knowing what he and his friends were setting out to do and more importantly; *why.* Leaving the house he quietly said, "Let's do it."

The *squirrel patrol* was assembled for a second time with a more definite approach. 'Round two' was about to unfold.

The evening continued with sporadic laughter flowing from the entertainment room. Nightfall arrived with John eventually returning home. Julia heard him enter the front door and went to see if he got his bounty. What she saw resembled something the cat would have drug in. It was her beloved brother with hair looking like it survived a hurricane. He was holding a bent fishing net with an empty cage.

Taking a step back she accessed the tattered mess. There was a multitude of grass stains running up one leg and continuing on the side of his face. A sleeve was partially torn matching the pant pocket just below.

There was more damage. Turning around, he placed the net and cage into the closet. With his backside exposed, the uncle now looked like a baseball player who slid into home plate. Facing Julia, his expression told the story. In disgust he limped towards the laundry room muttering, "I need to take a hot bath."

Leaving the score:

Humphrey–2

Humans–0

CHAPTER IX

The next morning Chase was with Justin as they entered the MCC. Chase wanted to have the honor of pushing Justin's wheelchair like he did the evening before around his neighborhood. Instead, Justin wanted the exercise and put on his special gloves to wheel himself.

"It's good to get some exercise once in a while," called out a voice. Looking to their right was the fatherly face of Andy Rutledge. He held up his hands showing that he also wore the same style of glove Justin wore. Pointing to Chase he added, "But it's always nice to have friends." That comment made Chase and Justin feel happy as they waved saying, "Good morning, Andy."

Andy's radiant personality responded. "Well, good morning, guys. Let's have a great day!"

"Okay," they replied.

It was apparent that The Meadowdale Community Center was starting off the week on a good note. The same, however, couldn't be said across town: Striker headquarters was throwing fits...

"This is outrageous!" cried out Mayor Warren Striker as he leaned back in his chair. Clenching the Meadowdale Review with both hands he continued to read. "What?" he asked out loud. "Who's making these claims, anyway?"

Paul Blades stood quietly before his uncle. The appointed aide always had the practice of scanning the morning paper as soon as it hit the stands. This was to give his uncle ample time to properly react to anything harmful directed at him. The morning's addition was devastating to say the least. The front headlines read:

"Meadowdale Rated Poorest Economy In State"

"Don't they realize what I've done for this town?" he questioned in a fury. Throwing the paper on his desk, he got up and paced the room. "Lies, all lies!" he exclaimed while pointing his index finger to the sky. The obedient nephew knew when to remain quiet. He just stood there watching his uncle's tantrum while nodding in agreement. "I'll show them," vowed Warren Striker in a loud voice as he raised his hook. He went behind his desk and sat down to read more.

Thumbing through the newsprint, he came across a few minor events that only a small town newspaper would cover. "No wonder they assassinate me," he said. "Why, this town has nothing better to do."

It was a moment of disparity for Warren Striker with his political career falling apart. Getting out of his chair he continued to pace the length of his office back and forth fighting the tears and searching for answers. Paul knew when to give his uncle space. "I'll be at my desk if you need anything," he said as he left the room, closing the door behind him.

Warren did need something; the company of a friend that would understand. One that didn't have any expectations and could give sound advice. A person that he didn't feel vulnerable around and could drop his guard. Until that weekend, no such person existed in the life of Warren Striker.

The mayor needed time to gather himself and lick his wounds. Once he acquired the necessary strength, he would call Peter and ask him out to lunch to discuss this important matter. A phone call that would change life in Meadowdale...

It was shortly before noon when Peter Constantine walked into the Main Street Cafe. Standing just inside the glass door, he scanned the room noticing a foursome of elder ladies sitting at a booth. Their mannerisms and hush-hush voice gave one the impression they were deeply enthralled in a conversation. Undoubtedly about a *friend* who wasn't present. Wisely, Peter tuned out the gossip and continued his search. In front of him was a man in a trench coat sitting at the counter. A closer look revealed gray hair and broad shoulders; disqualifying the suspect.

Peter concluded that he must have arrived first and looked for the nearest available table. At that moment, an inconspicuous motioning from a dark corner caught his attention. It was a short, heavy-set male whose face was partially covered by a tilted plaid hat. Under the brim was a pair of brown eyes with a twitching mustache peering over an open newspaper. A shiny hook waved at Peter confirming identification. It was his friend, Warren Striker incognito.

Peter saw the local celebrity acting out of character. Traditionally, the flamboyant mayor was never one to be unnoticed in public. This moment was different as if they were international spies trading information. The man with the eye patch leaned forward to better focus on the image before him. Bewildered, Peter looked around to see if any suspicious eyes were watching. Calmly, he walked up to Warren and sat in the chair facing him. Leaning forward, he whispered, "Is something wrong?"

"Did you see what they're doing to me?" came his response in a quivering voice. Warren turned the paper around displaying the incriminating headlines.

Peter already read that morning's paper. "I've already gone thru that," he said. "It's just that old American saying about *no news like bad news.*"

Warren sat up realizing that Peter believed in him and wanted to hear more.

"The truth of the matter is that the entire world is struggling to survive, and not just Meadowdale," said Peter. "You can only do the best you can for the situation given and that puts you at the same level where all of the other mayors are."

Warren was starting to feel better and asked, "Isn't there something we can do to exceed above the rest?"

"Certainly; you and I are military men," he said with confidence. "There's always a way."

That answer registered deep. Warren liked being put on Peter's level. He also liked the concept of having a plan that gave him control. "Any ideas?" he asked.

"Just an age-old battle plan that almost never fails," came his reply.

"And?" probed Warren.

Peter placed his elbows on the table. Methodically, he opened both hands and joined them together with only the thumbs and fingertips touching. Looking at Warren, he began to counsel. "Sometimes it's best to take the fight to the enemy."

The student nodded his head as Peter Constantine continued. "Governor Holland just took an offense against us. He is now waiting to see what our next move is going to be."

"What would you do?" asked Warren.

"I would challenge him by inviting he and his wife to this town and show what we have to offer," advised Peter. "You could even declare a 'Governor's Day' and celebrate him at city hall with the whole town invited."

Warren stood up and pointed at Peter. "That's a great idea!" he exclaimed. Sitting down, he added ideas of his own. "Every place of business, service and classroom could participate and have separate booths to represent who they are and what they do."

"Very good," encouraged Peter.

Warren Striker was on a roll. "The City Hall Auditorium would be filled with everyone wanting to meet the governor and shake his hand."

"Good, good..." commented Peter.

"Hot dogs, a band in our park and a tour throughout the town would open up his eyes," said Warren.

"That's what we want," said Peter. "He needs to see what we are presently doing and what we don't have."

Mayor Striker fully understood what Peter meant. "Right," he said. "I'll get together with my aide this afternoon and begin to lay out a plan."

"Let me know if there's anything I can do for you," offered Peter with sincerity.

"Oh, I will, Peter," said Warren. "Trust me, I will..."

Warren was a new man full of enthusiasm. Changing subjects he asked Peter, "Are you hungry?"

"I'm starving," he answered.

"I bet you're one of those guys who appreciates a good Reuben sandwich," speculated Warren in a happy tone.

"A Reuben Sandwich?" questioned Peter as he raised his hands in glory. "You mean that deli sandwich with tons of sauerkraut?" Looking directly at Warren he fallaciously asked, "Are you forgetting where I'm from? That's sounds perfect!"

"I have to agree," said Warren. "And this one's on me."

Peter's hindsight was just the right medicine. The 'buds' enjoyed lunch with Warren Striker being able to continue life in a positive direction.

An hour later Warren returned to his office and promptly got on the internet. He looked up the governor's publicly displayed schedule and saw that the last Saturday of the month was open. A vacancy that matched the lackluster town of Meadowdale. With cell phone in hand, he made his move and started dialing. After two rings a secretary answered the call singing her standard greeting, "Governor Holland's office."

Warren's forte was turning on the charm when needed. "Good morning," he replied in a vibrant tone. "This is Mayor Striker of Meadowdale. May I talk to Governor Holland if he's not too busy?"

There was a pause with the distinct flowing voice of Governor Holland himself being connected. "Warren, it's good to hear from you."

'Tic for tac' he replied, "It's good to hear you too, governor."

"It's *James* to you," carried the voice with a touch of humor. "Look," he said. "If this is about this morning's newspaper headline; I can explain..."

Warren had his boss where he wanted him. He already initiated a 'first name basis' and was apologetic to boot. Mayor Striker knew how to capitalize on such instances and chose the *humble approach.* "What are you talking about, James?" he asked. "I read the article and couldn't agree with you more." There was a pause with Warren Striker taking his assault to the next level.

"Our township is proud of who we are and have some wonderful things that represent us. We want to invite you and your lovely wife to Meadowdale the Saturday after next and join us for our 'Governor's Day Celebration.' Everyone here wants to meet you, show what their trade accomplishes and what their interests are. Many want to get their picture taken with you. Most importantly, you can see our town and suggest anything you see fit that could help the local economy."

There was a pause with the governor finally giving his response. "I'm flattered, Warren. My wife and I love this country and the many *Meadowdales* it's made up of. Why, we'd love to spend a day in your town and meet everyone."

"James, you've just made an entire town very happy," said Mayor Striker. "Can you and the misses drop by my office any time after twelve noon a week from this Saturday?"

"We'll be there at noon, and we're looking forward to spending the day with you," came Jame's reply. "See you there and thank you, Warren."

"I'm looking forward to seeing you two," he said gracefully. "And bring an empty stomach!"

"You can count on that," said the governor as he chuckled. "Bye, Warren."

"Bye, James," said Warren with the call ending.

Warren knew there was a lot to do and got on the intercom to summon his aide. The nephew responded, "Right away," and in seconds was standing at attention in front of his uncle.

The mayor looked at him with a smug look on his face. With hands clasped behind his head and feet up on his desk, he addressed the twenty-year-old. *"Sometimes you have to take the fight to the enemy..."*

CHAPTER X

That week fliers from the mayor's office reached every mailbox in the town of Meadowdale. It told of the upcoming Governor's Day Celebration and of the many family-oriented activities that would take place.

The MCC was just starting its morning session with Renée Klause addressing the room. "I have some *very* important news to share with the class today," she said.

The community circle gave their undivided attention as she continued. "We have received a message from the mayor's office and are asked to participate in the upcoming Meadowdale Governor's Day Celebration." The news was overwhelming with chests puffing out and heads turning to one-another. Dolly chimed in with a bark as she wagged her tail.

Renée glanced at the room with an expression of excitement. Taking a deep breath she continued. "It says here that we are being ask to set up a booth at the City Hall Auditorium to represent ourselves to the governor." In triumph, she waived the flier over her head stating, "Isn't this exciting?"

Faces beamed with pride with cheers echoing throughout the room. This was a victory for those who felt like a child pawned-off to a summer camp. It was now their turn to meet society on an even playing field and show who they really were. An opportunity that would set the world on fire.

"We can spend the next few days discussing how we want to represent ourselves," said Renée Swiftly, she changed topics and said, "But first, Andy wants to tell us something." Ella Ray took that as a cue and quietly got up and walked to the light switch.

Andy wasted no time putting an oversized party hat on his head and wheeling in front of the class. Ella turned out the lights as Andy's hat lit up with various flashing lights. "It's social time!" called out the jovial man as he spun erratically, giving a light show.

The surprised room cheered in approval with one golden retriever barking profusely. Soon Ella flicked the lights back on with Renée saying, "This would be a good time to share any ideas you might have about the Governor's Day Celebration." The tempo of the room was at an all-time high with friends savoring an array of treats with other friends. In time the words, "Hey, I have an idea," could be heard from all corners of the room.

After social hour was complete with everything clean and put away, Renée gave the order for the day. "Since it's nice outside, and we are caught up with our chores, we might as well pick up litter and meet our neighbors in the community." There was a touch of cabin fever in the room with everyone wanting to play outside that day.

Within twenty minutes, the members were across the street, working in twos. Dolly wore a saddle bag and made her rounds to allow others to empty their garbage sacks when needed. Chase wanted to spend his day with Andy. "Andy, do you mind if I work with you today?" asked Chase in a humble tone.

"Mind?" questioned Andy in a startled voice. "I was going to ask if you wouldn't mind working with *me* today." Chase loved being accepted by his friend and smiled. Andy looked beyond Chase and saw a paper cup that someone mindlessly threw on the ground.

Immediately a frown came across his face as he pointed towards it. "We can start right there." He rolled his wheelchair past Chase and towards the paper cup. Holding an extension with claw-like prongs, he worked a trigger-like handle on the opposite end. He opened the prongs and used them to grab the cup. "There," he said with satisfaction. He ingeniously attached a garbage bag to the side of his chair and in one motion, dropped the cup into the bag.

Chase marveled at how clever and resourceful the man was. He also admired on how he always applied those gifts to do *the right thing.*

Chase's mind was moving fast as he asked him a question. "Why do people litter?"

That question struck a nerve with Andy as he took a deep breath and closed his eyes. After a long pause he said, "That's a good question." Turning his chair towards Chase, he said, "I will never understand why people litter."

Chase shared the same sediments. "I saw a grownup drive down the street once and he threw a napkin out the window and kept driving."

That story was all-too common for Andy. Squinting his eyes, he looked at Chase and asked. "What did you do?"

"I picked it up and put it into our trash can," he said.

Andy smiled at Chase and said, "You know what?"

Chase concentrated on the question and asked, "What?"

"That's what I would have done," he replied. Andy extended his hand and gave a firm handshake to his equal.

Chase felt motivated and said, "Let's pick up as much litter as we can find today."

"I'm with ya," said Andy as he saluted him. The team scavenged about for any form of waste that could be seen. On occasion, a car would pass tooting its horn. "Do you hear that?" asked Andy. "People see what we're doing and like it!" The comment made Chase's face beam with pride and compelled him to work at a more frantic pace. Andy laughed to himself and did his best to keep up.

Soon Dolly was rubbing her side against Chase. "Wow!" said Renée "You have picked up more litter than everyone else put together. I brought some juice; why don't you two take a break?"

"That sounds good," said Andy. "We appreciate this." Andy and Chase took a much-needed rest and enjoyed a cup of grape juice.

In the meanwhile, Renée emptied their trash bags into the larger saddlebags that Dolly carried. Soon Renée left to serve other teams as Andy and Chase got back to work.

Their day would eventually have a picnic at a nearby park, with the crew later going back to work. Their entire day was dedicated to serving the community and meet as many people as possible.

Chase was having an inspiring day with an evening at Justine's to look forward to.

Later that evening the 'squirrel patrol' was having another briefing before battle. The meeting took place in John Mansfield's back yard and was of a more sophisticated manner. Each member had agreed to do some research in order to understand more about their prey.

"The *sciuridae* family has 278 species," said Steve Smith with a raised eyebrow.

John also spent some time on the computer and had something to add. "The Greek word, *Skiouros* and the New Latin word, *morpha* mean: a nearly cosmopolitan family of

sciuromorpha rodents consisting of true squirrels, ground squirrels, marmots and related rodents."

Allen was well-prepared and made his contribution: "They are a docile creature that usually feeds on nuts, seeds, conifer cones, fruits, fungi and green vegetation." Three heads nodded in understanding as their education expanded.

John seemed to be their self-appointed leader and converted his backyard into a training camp. He made a squirrel-size object out of wood that rolled on four wheels. An old wire brush was nailed upright in the back to resemble Humphrey. A nail was sticking out of the front with a string tied to it. John explained that since the rodent is also an animal; it makes it *unpredictable.* Each was to take turns pulling the makeshift rodent in an unorthodox way as to give a last-second direction change, while the others tried to net it. This would improve their eye-hand coordination in the art of catching a squirrel in the wild.

A voice interrupted the training. "What are you guys doing?" asked Chase as he stood on the back deck holding a small cage.

His uncle, John was startled and momentarily at a loss for words. Noticing that Chase was holding a cage he asked, "Hey, what do you have in there?"

"Humphrey," responded the nephew.

"Humphrey?" asked Steve in a high voice.

"Sure," said Chase. "Come over and take a look at him."

The patrol did just that and saw a tiny nose sniffing at the mesh screen that enclosed it. The chopped tail and bulging brown eyes were the proof in the pudding.

"How did you catch it?" asked the curious uncle.

"Justine and I took the screen off of the cage and turned it up-side-down. We then used a stick to hold up one end and placed some nuts under the cage. Justine tied a string to the stick and when Humphrey came to get the nuts, pulled on it and trapped him."

John, Steve and Allen looked up into the vast universe and pieced together the information just given. There was a moment of silence until Steve spoke up. "Where did you get that idea from?"

Chase had an immediate answer. "We saw the roadrunner catch the coyote that way."

CHAPTER XI

C hase Mansfield finished his bedtime prayers as his mother kissed him on the forehead. Upon being tucked in bed, he asked her a question. "Do you think Humphrey missed me?"

"Why, yes," she said. "He missed you very much."

"Then why did he take so long to come to me?" he asked.

"Because he wanted to make sure that all of his friends had enough food before he left to be with you," she explained in a motherly tone.

Chase turned and looked at the cage that rested on his nightstand. Inside he could see his furry friend curled up in a ball and fast asleep. It was now just a matter of time until a suitable home would be found for the disfigured squirrel. A home that would have its house numbers displayed by 'Sparkles' so that Humphrey would always find his way. "I'm sure glad he's here," said Chase.

"We all are," replied his mother. "Just remember that all people need to be loved and wanted."

That comment registered deep with Chase as more concerns came to surface. "Like the people who live where grandma lives?"

"That's right," she said. Julia kissed her son on the cheek and said, "It's time to sleep now. I'll turn off the light and have a good breakfast waiting for you in the morning. Good night, Chase."

"Good night, mom."

Julia left the room and turned off the light before closing the door. Chase was now alone with Humphrey and started to think about the many others that needed to be rescued. He remembered his recent visit at the Meadowdale Retirement Home and playing checkers with his new friend, Harvey. The eighty-eight year-old left a firm impression in Chase's mind when he said: *"Aging often means having fewer people in one's life."* Chase recalled how that comment reminded him of the many pets he saw earlier that day at the animal shelter.

He fell asleep with his conscience reaching out to those lonely souls that needed to be exposed. His dream took place in the animal shelter with his grandmother, Harvey and many other seniors being locked in cages. They, along with the many animals incarcerated there were all begging to be released. Chase opened the cages and watched them roll, hobble and run outside. He followed the stampede and saw that Humphrey was leading them towards a monstrous image of Sparkles, the feeder he made at the MCC. It was obvious to him that they were all being freed and led to their salvation.

Chase tossed and turned until waking up in a cold sweat. He had no doubt that he was to interpret his dream as an assignment.

———

The next day found Chase sitting next to Andy during social time. The regal man in the wheelchair detected a worrisome look on Chase's face and asked, "Is there something wrong?"

Chase's intense blue eyes pierced Andy's heart as he began to speak. "Andy, do you remember when you said that one day we could have a field trip to the beach to get things for our artwork?"

"Yes, I remember that," he said.

"Can we have a field trip to visit the old people at the retirement home instead?" he asked.

"Sure," he replied. "We can do both." Andy sensed an urgency in Chase's voice and asked, "When would you like to do that?"

Chase's eyes grew with excitement as he replied, "Can we do it now?"

"Possibly," he answered in a calm voice. "May I ask why?"

Chase knew that he could talk to his older friend and shared with him what he learned from visiting the retirement home. He discussed the conversations he had with his mother, uncle, grandmother and others about how lonely and forgotten such people are.

"At this very moment they are waiting there, hoping that someone, *anyone* would at least come by to say, "Hi," to them," the boy

stressed. He elaborated further and talked about the many lost pets in the shelter. "They all need to be held and taken to a new home," he said with emotion.

A tear trickled down Andy's eye with him saying, "You're right." He wheeled away and was soon having a private conversation with Renée and Julia. Soon both women were nodding their heads with looks of astonishment. Andy rolled backwards several feet and immediately made a few calls on his cell phone.

Julia was heading class that day and walked to the front of the room saying, "I'd like to have everyone's attention for a minute." All eyes were on her as she gave the announcement. "Chase Mansfield has brought to our attention that we have neighbors that we are overdue to visit," she said. Julia went on to tell everyone that arrangements were being made for the MCC to visit the Meadowdale Retirement Center and the animal shelter that day. "We'll even supply lunch for everyone," she added.

Once again everyone looked at Chase Mansfield with admiration. "Do they know that we're coming?" he asked.

"No they don't," answered Andy. "It's okay for neighbors to drop in on one-another on occasion. We'll just consider ourselves as the 'welcome wagon' making the first move."

Soon, Andy's personal bus pulled up in the parking lot with a duplicate following behind. Like the one he arrived in every day, both had wheelchair access. The buses were also staff by crews who wore sharp outfits and displayed expertise in assisting the handicapped.

There always seemed to be a touch of magic when it came to Andy Rutledge. The middle-aged man who dressed sensible always had a smile for everyone. He seemed to like others *as if he needed them,* taking into account everything they had to say. And then, like a rabbit being pulled out of a hat, *made things happen.*

The concept of traveling first-class was a 'never before heard of ' treat for the MCC. From the initial touch of being greeted by professional chauffeurs, to the special care that accompanied the luxurious ride, it was royalty at its finest. Today, those who represented the MCC would reach out to the Meadowdale Retirement Home, arriving with a well-deserved celebrity status.

Andy's voice could be heard through each driver's radio saying, "Let's make a nice scenic drive out of this." The high-class caravan would take in the many sites throughout town, turning heads as they rode. Many pointed at the charter with seniors, handicapped and those of special needs waving back. It was the ride of their life, with each passenger feeling *important.*

The best was yet to come. They would have an eye-opening experience by discovering that the retirement center was another struggling facility; one that had much in common with the MCC. It too, was a community that could relate to the causes Chase and his friends championed.

The motorized parade entered the parking lot of The Meadowdale Retirement Home. Immediately, tired faces came to life as they peered through windows and left to summon others. Before the buses were emptied many were watching with canes raised and hands waving. It was obvious that their unannounced visit was welcomed.

As an extra touch, a catering truck from Louie's Deli pulled in with more than enough food to feed an entire retirement center. It was 'East meeting West' as open arms shuffled out from the main doors greeting their visitors. Chase was overwhelmed watching the friendly exchange take place with those crying for joy. He felt a nudge against his leg and turned to see his friend, Harold grinning at him. "This time I'm gonna beat you in checkers," said the crafty old man.

Another confrontation came from his opposite side. "Chase, I thought that was you." The recognizable voice was non-other than his grandma, Becky. He was accosted affectionately by her hugging arms and warm kiss on his cheek.

Another unexpected brush surprised the boy that almost made him lose his balance. It was Andy wheeling by as he patted him on the back saying, "This is a great idea, Chase." The retirement center was now the hotspot in town. Every seat was taken; every game was being played with introductions and stories running rampid. Sandwiches from the town's best deli along with chips and drinks created a Thanksgiving all in its own.

There was more.

Andy made arrangements to bus the residents to the Meadowdale Animal Shelter as a way to *get them out*. It also allowed them to make more friends.

The result?

"Mork" and "Mindy," the most senior cats from the shelter, were adopted by Valery Tomkins. The center's volunteer receptionist had the connections to admit *anyone* she saw fit to live there. The felines would go on to become the most popular residents at the Meadowdale Retirement Home. Their day would consist of playing with yarn, sitting on laps, and the occasional nip of catnip when nobody was looking. The pair would also have their choice of any room to spent the night in and cuddle up with a loved one.

The three-ring circus had non-stop activity throughout the day. It was like a square dancing marathon with everyone constantly exchanging partners. Eventually, the topic about the upcoming Governor's Day Celebration was brought up. "We heard about it," said a spunky eighty-three-year-old Katie Kaiser. "But we really wouldn't have anything to show the governor."

Renée Klause took over. "You'll have plenty to show if you join us at the MCC and do arts and crafts with us."

"Can anyone go?" asked seventy-nine-year-old Wilbur Fish as he rested in his wheelchair.

Andy was present and got Wilbur's attention. "*Anyone* can go," he stressed.

"We can have our display booths together and put on a fabulous presentation," said Renée It was soon coordinated that the buses out front could be used every day to transport anyone from the retirement center to the MCC. It was also understood that, like the MCC, the Meadowdale Retirement Home also had an 'open door policy' every day of the year.

Handshakes, hugs, and phone numbers dwindled down the visit as the guests said their goodbyes and boarded the bus.

That day was a milestone. It greatly expanded the MCC and knocked down the inhumane wall of isolation for the retirement home. In short: everyone got a little younger that day with hope having finally arrived. Chase Mansfield's compassion for others was credited for this monumental event, but there was another player.

Andy seemed to be the one who snapped his finger and put things in motion. The man in the wheelchair who mysteriously showed up one day in a million dollar travel bus. He was pleasant in demeanor and always performed with a warm, professional touch. Andy was comfortable to be around and fit in perfectly. There was still, however a question hovering over his head.

Who is Andy Rutledge?

CHAPTER XII

The Governor's Day event was just five days away with the MCC getting their gun loaded.

Ella Ray and Louis Sexton took into account of the many that were expected to join that day. They more than doubled the baked goods that they usually brought. Steve Smith was also concerned about a 'treat shortage' and brought more utensils and an extra gallon of punch. Renée baked a large sheet cake with "Welcome To The Meadowdale Community Center" written across the top in red frosting.

At the Meadowdale Retirement Home, a *counter attack* was being planned.

Those who lived there were taken by the love and generosity displayed by the MCC. It was now their turn to flex their muscle. Cakes, pies and cookies were being carried onto the bus by the new recruits. In moments, over fifty seniors would enter the MCC led by a lone man in a wheelchair: Andy Rutledge.

Upon entering the homeroom, arms extended wide-opened to embrace a new friend they recognized. The dessert table couldn't sustain the many treats that were brought causing a card table to be rushed into service. Laughter, along with more introductions and an overly excited dog would kick the day off. Soon an expanded circle was formed with Steve and Allen Smith sharing duties to lead class. Those who were new could sense that something 'out of the norm' was about to happen and watched with curiosity.

Steve started class by addressing the congregation. "The first thing in order is to welcome our friends from the Meadowdale Retirement Home and thank them for being here with us today." A huge response came from the original MCC members with a thunderous applause that almost shook the room. Once the ovation died down, Steve's face became one of a serious expression, possessing a look that seemed to command laughter. His son, Allen gave the same expression with each walking to the center of the circle.

"There's something that we need to share with this room," said Allen in a serious tone. The father and son team reached into their pockets and all at once yelled, "It's social hour!" Immediately they threw glitter confetti up in the air and grabbed more out of their pockets. They threw it in all directions as they ran around the room. The newcomers were greatly amused with cheers and whistles approving their actions. Dolly was going bonkers!

Andy made a brief announcement on behalf of the new members and explained to them what 'social hour' was. He then requested they form a line to be served first. The room resembled the recent event they had at the retirement home, with everyone holding a plate full of goodies and mingling.

The influx of new members had social hour run for almost two hours. Steve, Allen and Chase efficiently cleaned up afterwards with the circle being re-established. It was time to have an open floor discussion. The topic would be about the Governor's Day Celebration with any thoughts or ideas encouraged to be shared.

Gretta Heims wasn't shy and raised her hand. Everyone present showed courtesy and motioned towards her to speak. "We are excited about being included with The Governor's Day Celebration," said the seventy-six-year-old with a walker. "We just don't know what to do."

Renée responded in a comforting voice. "Gretta," she said. "We have a great art room here with everyone helping everyone. Why don't you and I work together today? We can add flowers, ribbons and paint pictures on your hat and purse so that they match with a special distinction. We can then display it as a joint project that we did together."

Gretta's face lit up. She loved the idea of dressing up her hat and purse; just like the dolls she played with when she was a child. "I'd love that so-much!" she said in a quivering voice.

More people from the retirement home spoke up. It seemed that they *all* wanted to work with the MCC and show their colors to the governor. Soon the art room was packed with projects being started. Paintings, watercolors and sculptures led the pack. The idea of restoring old chairs, tables and touching up antique vases to hold flowers was also in the making.

———

Across town, Peter Constantine was in a closed conference with Mayor Striker.

"Good, good," said Peter as he paced in front of Warren's desk looking at the floor. Instantaneously he turned around and pointed his index finger at the mayor and asked, "What if he tells you a joke?"

Warren was doing 'so-far, so-good' on his interrogation and gave his answer. "I laugh at it."

"How do you laugh at it?" asked Peter.

The former used car salesman needed no rehearsal. "Like this," said Warren. He stood up from his chair and changed his face into one of elation. Squinting his eyes, he covered up his stomach with both hands and said, "Governor Hastings, that's the funniest thing I'd ever heard." Standing up straight with a blank stare, he asked, "Like that?"

"Yes, like that," said Peter.

The man of Bavarian ancestry continued to pace as more thoughts festered out of his mind. Spinning around, he pointed again at Warren. "If he tells you his golf score?"

Without a thought, Warren gave his answer. "I let him know that his is better than mine."

"How much better?" asked Peter with his lone eye squinting.

"Much better," came his response.

"Very good," said Peter as he resumed pacing.

Peter stopped and looked at Warren. "Have you decided on what you're going to be wearing?"

"I just bought a new suit and had it tailored," he said.

"Wrong," said Peter.

"Wrong?" asked Warren.

Peter Constantine stepped towards him and placed his palms firmly on the desk. "Why?" asked Peter in a facetious tone. "Because he knows that you are going to put your best foot forward. If that's the case, show him that you have been financially diminished to thrift stores and have a dignity about it. Get it?" he coached.

Warren looked away to digest the concept. Looking back, he nodded, saying, "I get it."

"There's lots of talk out on the streets about the Governor's Day Celebration," said Peter. "It appears that the whole town will be involved which is what you want. I would spend the rest of the week walking around and shaking hands," advised Peter.

"Will do," said Warren as he saluted his hook.

"I have a plumber coming to my house today, so I need to go," informed Peter. "If you have the time, let's meet for dinner this week."

"That would be great," he said, "and thanks."

The week was fast and furious in the town of Meadowdale with everyone getting ready for the governor's arrival.

Spaces in the City Hall Auditorium were going fast with the MCC making the first claim. They elected to set up a colossal stand in the far left corner of the hall. It was a way to respect others by occupying the furthest area. Their display would be a joint-effort with The Meadowdale Retirement Home.

Throughout the week, the MCC worked at a pace that could keep up with Santa's workshop. Finished projects were promptly sent to the City Hall Auditorium and arranged in their showcase. The harmony was inspiring with those who finished first, immediately offering a hand to others.

By Friday, the *new* MCC was at the City Hall Auditorium giving the finishing touch to their display. Or so they thought...

Purple and pink ribbons gracefully outlined the display. A sign with beautiful patriotic writing hung above, reading:

The Meadowdale Community Center
and
Retirement Home
Welcomes Governor Hastings!

Fresh flowers from the retirement home's garden adorned restored vases. Artwork, small statues, and a collage of pictures showing the members working on projects were spread throughout in a uniformed pattern. Gretta Heims' refurbished hat and purse were proudly displayed along with canes, chairs and other pieces of furniture showing off their new gleam. Renée and the entire membership stood back and marveled at what they had accomplished. In a sing-song voice she said, "I think we're about done."

Chase intervened by correcting her. "We're not done yet."

All present heard what he said and looked at him with dumbfounded expressions. "What do you mean?" asked Renée.

"We need to have the animal shelter here," he protested. "They belong with us."

Chase was right with everyone realizing it. At that moment, eyes wandered around showing embarrassment. "Chase is right again," said Andy. "Let's go to the animal shelter and get some pets in here!"

"I'll help," said Wilbur Fish.

"I want to go too," said Katie Kaiser.

"Make room for me!" said Lois Sexton.

An hour later they returned with twelve caged residents from the Meadowdale Animal Shelter. A pyramid consisting of six cages surrounded the sides of the display like bookends. Renée went to work and made signs for each cage that read:

"I want to go home with you."

"Please take me!"

"I've been waiting all my life for you."

"I love you."

There were also name tags for each pet placed above its cage. The joyous sounds of meows and barks drew attention far and wide. Wagging tails with furry faces rubbing against metal screens encouraged all to come closer. Innocent eyes of hope would soon break hearts and fine new homes.

It was obvious that many would be adopted with volunteers ready to bring replacements *on the double.*

The banner was taken down and modified.

It was soon put back, reading:

The Meadowdale Community Center
Retirement Home
and
Animal Shelter
Welcomes Governor Hastings!

There was also an extra bonus thrown into the works. Recently, an African Amazon Parrot had been donated to the Meadowdale Animal Shelter. A talking species with a lifespan of over fifty years. It was just shy of its twenty-fifth birthday, having lived with various families throughout the community. This lime green and yellow bird with red highlights was caged near the front desk and considered to be part of the staff. It was agreed that "Jayde" and Humphrey would be added to their display to greet people, but *not* to be adopted.

There was more to this pet.

Jayde had a unique history that one might find amusing. It was the product of being perched in living rooms with an uncanny knack for absorbing specific commercials and news events from television sets. It also had a recall on the many derogatory comments made about them. Cute jingles, breaking news and fits from disgusted family members were all delivered with an impeccable sense of timing.

Can we say, "Striker Motors?"

CHAPTER XIII

The big day arrived with Warren in his office standing in front of a full-length mirror. The brown suit that he wore years ago was tight in a few places with a style that dated himself. Slowly he turned around, stretching and twitching to get his best fit.

A voice startled him. "You look the part."

Turning to his left was his friend, Peter, sitting in a chair. "I tapped on the door and it opened, so I knew it was okay to come in. How do you feel?"

"Nervous," replied the mayor as he straightened his tie.

"You'll do just fine," assured Peter. "Just remember that he must see you as someone who idolizes him and wants to be just like him."

"That I can do," said Warren winking back.

Peter was giving his final briefing. "Where and when do you meet the governor and his wife?"

"We talked on the phone last night and agreed to meet at the gazebo just outside of this building," he said.

"Nice touch," complimented Peter. "Then what?"

"We will watch the parade together, look at the vintage car show that will follow and then go to the City Auditorium to see the exhibits."

"Friend," said Peter. "Do yourself a favor and walk through the auditorium before meeting them; just to make sure."

"Gotcha," said Warren as he gave a thumbs-up.

"I must go now," said Peter. "I have volunteered to be on a few committees today, so my dance card is full."

"I appreciate all that you do for this town and for me," said Warren.

"You're worth it, friend," said Peter as they shook hands. The man with the eye patch promptly left with Mayor Warren Striker sitting down and taking a deep breath.

A last-minute survey was taking place at the MCC to assure that no project remained behind. Renée, Julia and John walked through all rooms and looked into closets. All seemed in order until Renée went into the art room one last time and entered a walk-in closet that was partially hidden.

Turning on the light she saw a friendly mechanical face looking back. It was 'Sparkles' with a look that matched its counterparts at the animal shelter. *"Well, you'll just have to come with us,"* she thought to herself. With loving care, Renée picked up the three-legged spaceman and carried it out to the bus. Within a half hour, it was standing in its rightful place with Jayde, Humphrey and a dozen orphans waiting to put on a show. Dolly was there in full force carrying her saddle bags with signs welcoming the governor and his wife to Meadowdale. A patriotic hat with matching sunglasses made the canine's outfit complete.

Mayor Striker had gathered his composure and left for the hall. Once inside he took a giant step backwards in awe. Before him were many displays that illustrated Meadowdale's pride. Each gave a well thought-out presentation of who they were and what they did. All had festive signs welcoming the governor.

Mayor Warren Striker was proud.

They were all a 'labor of love' with each holding its own character. The mayor swiftly inspected each booth waving his trademark hook and shaking hands. As he neared the back, the playful sounds of people, cats, dogs and a singing parrot were becoming more prevalent. He was now entering a community all of its own. The playfulness increased in pitch until he was standing in front of it. Staring at him would be the recipient of every blue ribbon to be awarded that day.

In fact, it was Chase Mansfield himself who went on to receive not one, but two of the most prized ribbons. His creation of Sparkles had received a unanimous vote for both *Most Creative* and *Most Popular Entree.* Chase even went on to have his picture printed on the front page of The Meadowdale Gazette with Humphrey and Sparkles.

This was the Meadowdale Community Center, Retirement Home and Animal Shelter exhibit. It was the only section of the auditorium that had something for everyone; because it *included* everyone.

There were magnificent paintings and finger paintings signed by the artists. Antique items were restored and covered with lively colors. There were even baked goods along with jams and jellies; free for the taking. Most of all, it utilized everyone who was a part of it with happy faces introducing themselves. This section was also accompanied with a variety of shiny noses, whiskers, one beak, a roving dog incognito and a visit from an alien-type looking friend.

This was a wonderland *everyone* wanted to be a part of.

Setting up the monumental display took its toll with Andy offering to treat everyone at a concession stand. Nobody argued. They all left, allowing Warren to spend a few minutes alone and study the many intricate facets that the three facilities assembled. One-by-one he smiled at each cat and dog wishing he could pet them. He spent an extra moment looking at *Chelsey,* an affectionate long-hair calico cat. Its beautiful, bright orange, white and black fur would soon be sitting on someone's lap in her new home; purring with gratitude. Next to Chelsey was, Goldie. A lively golden-orange cat that would soon find a home with a loving family.

With hand and hook behind his back, he gazed up and down as he walked from one side to the other. Eventually, he peered into Jayde's cage, with the colorful Amazon staring back. The parrot's eyes began to dilate as if to identify Warren. Taking a deep breath it called out, "Brrrraak, Striker Motors at 411 Main Street."

The former used car salesman involuntarily stood up feeling the recognition of celebrity status. Hoping that others heard the comment, he looked side to side while straightening his tie. Looking back, he leaned closer and said, "Yeah, that was me."

Jayde's eyes dilated more as it took another deep breath. Staring directly at Warren it blasted, "Striker's a crook! I want my money back. Brrrraak!"

It took only a micro-second for a startled Warren Striker to looked all directions. He breathed easier discovering that no one heard the accusation.

With a stunned look, he hunched towards the bird and placed his index finger in front of his mouth. "Shhhhhh," was the soft sound he made in an attempt to quiet the tropical pet.

Jayde's yellow head turned while maintaining eye contact with the parrot taking another deep breath. Warren started to use both hands in a surrender mode, pleading for Jayde to keep silent. It was to no avail as the African parrot bellowed, "News at eleven." The man was relieved believing that the talking bird changed its *repetiteur* until it recited, "Get a job, Striker!"

In a flimsy-type fashion, he sporadically danced as if being electrocuted. Looking around, he was thankful to see that it was all in private. Warren noticed a clock on the wall and saw it was time to meet the governor and his wife. The mayor left in anguish shaking his head. With hook and hand pressed against his face, he muttered, *"Who taught that bird to talk?"*

Once outside the mayor noticed how immaculate his town was. Everything was clean and orderly with an air of excitement. It would have made the perfect setting for a Hallmark movie. Looking ahead, he saw a well-dressed couple standing next to the gazebo.

The man was tall, graced with regal silver hair and had a distinct handsome face. His black suit was the best money could buy and was accented with a smart white shirt and blue silk tie. The woman was beautiful with stunning shoulder-length blonde hair. Her blue silk dress matched the man's tie with their eyes appearing identical. It was unmistakably the governor and his wife, Stephanie.

Warren Striker knew plenty about Governor Hastings. He was a good caring man that did everything possible for the state. He did, however possess a back-home country twang that had been known to dictate his actions. Numerous times this character trait had surfaced, reducing him to an invincible 'cornball.'

Warren was prepared and approached them. "I hope I didn't keep you two waiting," he said in an apologetic tone.

Governor James Hastings turned around projecting a genuine smile. "Warren, it's great to see you!" he said extending his hand. Shaking hands, the governor turned to his wife. "You know my wife, Stephanie, don't you?"

Warren Striker's charm was in high gear. "Nobody could ever forget meeting your wife," he said. "You look wonderful today, Stephanie."

"Thank you, Warren," she said giving a hug.

Looking at James Hastings, he continued, "And so do you, governor."

"Please," said Governor Hastings, "Call me, James."

"James it is!" laughed Warren. "Hey, the people of this town want to meet you and we also have our musicians performing. How about you and the misses taking a little tour with me?"

"We'd love that," said Stephanie.

James was elated over what was taking place and dropped his guard. He noticed a circular table that centered the gazebo and pointed at it. "Warren, do you know why I never eat at a round table?"

Mayor Striker acted curiously and, with a serious expression, asked, "Why?"

"Because I can't get a square meal!" he replied while laughing at his own joke.

Warren Striker always carried a cross for his lackluster military career. He also came within inches from being indicted as a used car salesman. Where he once failed as a soldier and entrepreneur, he would now make up for by serving his home town. Sucking it all in, he would now give his best performance. His eyes got large as he broke out laughing. Next he doubled-up, holding his stomach. "Did you come up with that on your own?" he asked between breaths. "You're killing me, James!" Warren remained bent over as if he went into a seizure.

"The barber shop in our neighbor thinks that James should try being a stand-up comedian when he retires," said Stephanie.

"He will pack the house!" said a teary-eyed Warren as he recovered from the first salvo.

James loved what he heard and beamed with pride. "I can hear some folk music," he said. "Let's get out there and meet everyone."

"Great idea," said Warren. "Follow me."

Mayor Striker's work was cut out for him that day. He would guide the governor through the day's events starting off by listening to local musicians. From there, he would join the couple in a Model T Ford and ride in the parade with the celebrated governor being grand marshal. Later, they would take in the local car show and watch the many games and events running ramped throughout the street fair. Lastly, they would see the exhibits in the City Hall Auditorium and have dinner at the local restaurant of his choice.

The trio had an exceptionally good day while many shook hands and got their picture taken with the governor. James Hastings was in his glory, except for when it came to those who obviously didn't have a sense of humor or lacked the capacity to understand his jokes.

Mayor Warren Striker held a good batting average as well with only a few hecklers directing their comments at him. Each attack was brushed off as *just an old friend playing,* with Mayor Striker waving back in a friendly manner. The governor and his wife were very observant with James commenting, "Everyone sure seems to know who you are." How right he was...

The day's schedule had gone according to plan with the exhibits in the City Hall Auditorium next in line. It was overwhelming for the governor and his wife to see the many booths that had signs and banners that personally greeted them. The Meadowdale police, fire and water department were just the tip of the iceberg. Every local business, club and service was present with all celebrating Governor Hastings. Handshakes with an occasional joke kept pace with the tour.

Combing their way towards the back, a loud whistling could be heard. "Is that a parrot?" asked Mrs. Hastings.

Warren heard the whistle and discretely left his guests. He made a beeline straight to the bird with it recognizing him. Taking a deep breath, it projected, "Brrraaakk, Striker Motors, 411 Main Street." Standing next to Jayde was Maria Rodriguez, apparently watching over the prized African Amazon parrot. Warren approached her out of breath and asked, "Is that your parrot?"

Maria recognized the mayor and said, "Well, not exactly. I am probably the one who takes care of it though."

"Can I buy it?" he asked.

"Jayde is not for sale," she said.

In desperation he pulled out his wallet and said, "Look, I'll give you twenty bucks for it."

Maria was feeling uncomfortable and said, "It belongs to the Meadowdale Animal Shelter and is not for sale."

"Warren raised his sleeve, showing a wrist watch. " Look, I'll throw this in," he begged. "It only needs a battery."

"No, I can't do that," replied Maria. "I can't sell Jayde to anyone."

Jayde chimed in, "News at eleven, bbrraaakk!"

"Can I ask you a favor?" asked Warren.

"Sure," replied Maria.

"There is a group of people at the Meadowdale Historical Society booth. They love the parrot and ask if you wouldn't mine taking it over to them for a while."

Maria saw no harm in the request and said, "Sure." The caring woman knew where the booth was and promptly picked up the caged bird. The transition did not come without incident. Jayde had the last word by calling out, "I want my money back, bbrraaakk!" The coast was clear with the trio having already visited the Historical Society's display. At that time, his guests rounded a corner and were walking towards him.

"So there you are," said the governor.

Looking at the three-in-one project Stephanie said, "Wow, they saved the best for last."

This display was different with the Hastings' being mesmerized at what they saw. It was laced with a huge population of seniors and disadvantaged that wore bright pastel shirts with their names printed on it. Shirts that Andy Rutledge provided that day.

They were all happy introducing themselves while offering homemade treats. The pyramid of caged pets that occupied both sides of the display served as a revolving door. Cats and dogs were constantly being chosen for adoption with replacements quickly filling their spots. Dolly still wore her hat and sunglasses while displaying her signs for the governor. "Oh, isn't that cute," said Stephanie.

Numerous artwork reached out to all, emphasizing the pride of the MCC. Just when an improvement was considered impossible, Sparkles was noticed.

Governor Hastings and his wife were almost in a trance when they spotted the feeder that stood before them. Its Martian-type, innocent face stared back with a compliment of food being gifted to any animal that was hungry or thirsty.

Stephanie's mouth opened in awe as she moved closer to it. Turning at the mayor she asked a question that would start a trend near and far:

"Where can I get one of these?"

CHAPTER XIV

The following Monday had the MCC practically overflowing. It yielded its highest turn-out with those outside searching for available parking. Inside, Chase was overwhelmed by the masses and asked Andy a question. "Why are there so many people here today?"

"They liked the display we had for the Governor's Day Celebration and wanted to be a part of us," said Andy.

Chase felt honored as he scanned the latest addition to the MCC. At that moment, he was addressed by someone standing next to him. "Hi, Chase," greeted a lean boy with short, black hair and prescription glasses.

Chase turned and saw Earl Gains smiling at him. Earl was a friend he made last summer at a church outing. The fifteen-year-old was challenged like Chase and lived in another town. "Can I be with you today?" he asked.

Chase was pleasantly surprised. He thought about Earl almost every day and wished he lived closer. "Earl, it's a lot of fun here!" Chase proclaimed. "Stay with me and I'll show you everything." He led Earl to the homeroom and found a place for them to sit down. "Make sure that we have enough room for Andy," he said pointing at his friend in the wheelchair.

Soon the three were together with Andy introducing himself. "My name is, Andy," he said extending his hand. "Chase is right," he added. "It is a lot of fun around here. Pleasure to meet you, Earl."

Earl was where he wanted to be. The special needs student always looked up to Chase and wanted to have more friends just like him. The boy eagerly shook hands and asked, "Are you my friend?"

Andy generated a warm smile that gave assurance. "Yes I am," he replied.

———————

Meanwhile at Striker headquarters, a private post-Governor's Day Celebration conference was taking place. Is was limited to Peter Constantine and Mayor Warren Striker as they hashed over the events that took place. Their objective was to unveil any opportunities that spawned from it.

It was the usual scenario with Striker sitting at his desk and Constantine looking down, pacing back and forth with hands behind back. They methodically walked through the chain of events from the time the governor and his wife arrived; until their departure.

Every trivial piece of information that entered their mind was discussed. "Governor Hastings likes to tell jokes and considers being a stand-up comic one day," said Warren. "Do we want to bill him as a successful comedian and sell tickets for him to perform here?"

Peter's face looked as if he just bit into a lemon. He was one of many that heard his monologue and commented, "I don't think there is enough alcohol in this state to pull that off."

It was of no laughing matter. "I have to agree," said the mayor.

It seemed that nothing would come of the celebration until Warren mentioned something in passing. "Boy, you should have seen the Governor's wife when she saw that squirrel feeder the Mansfield Boy made."

The comment stopped Peter in his tracks. Looking at Warren he said, "Tell me more..."

"Did you see any of the exhibits in the City Hall Auditorium?" asked the man behind the desk.

"I made it through just before it closed," he said.

"Did you see the last exhibit with that annoying parrot?" asked Warren.

"If you're talking about the one sponsored by the community center, retirement home and animal shelter, I did when the crowd finally thinned out," said Peter. "They stole the show."

"Did you notice that spaceman-type animal feeder they had there?" asked Warren.

"See it?" asked Peter in an astonishing tone. "I got in line to have my picture taken with it." He pulled out his cell phone and quickly showed the photo.

"That's the one," said the mayor. Holding up the morning's newspaper he pointed out, "Look, it made the front page of the Gazette. The governor's wife fell in love with it and asked me if she can get one." Warren placed the paper back down.

Peter was leading Warren and asked, "And you said?"

"I told her that there would be no problem getting her one since everything in that auditorium was a product from Meadowdale."

"Very good," commended Peter. "We've found what we were looking for!"

"What do you mean?" asked the mayor in a curious tone.

"Don't you see?" replied Peter as he reached for a chair. Sliding it to the front of the desk, he turned it backwards and straddled it. With arms folded on the backrest, he leaned towards his friend he said, "It's all there."

"Walk me through this," asked Warren as he laid back in his chair. Clasping his hands behind his head, he gave Peter his undivided attention.

Peter positioned his eye closer to the mayor and began to speak. "The Governor's Day Celebration was a reconnaissance mission to gather information needed to help Meadowdale. We learned that his wife likes something she saw, and that's all we need to know. The iron is hot, so we will take the fight to them a second time by inviting them back and presenting a feeder of their own."

Peter continued.

"That feeder was a personal item that meant something special to that boy. I will do a little research on the governor and find out what his interests are. We will then have the community center build a feeder that specifically pertains to the governor's interest. It's lightning in a bottle!" he exclaimed.

Peter stood up saying, "And that, my friend, will put us on the top of his list."

Warren looked at Peter like a child trying to grasp a concept. "You mean that we invite them over and hand them a gift?"

"Not exactly," said Peter. "It needs to be another dramatic presentation that emphasizes how special they are to us. One where they are put up in our best hotel and taken to our best restaurant. This could become a package for those who want a personalized feeder, with the customer spending a day or two here in the process."

Warren gazed towards the ceiling understanding what Peter said. Looking back, he raised his hook and said, "I like it."

Peter was in charge and sat back down. "Now, let's go through this. Do you have any problem putting the governor and his wife up in a hotel and taking them out for a meal?"

Warren imagined on how such an event would take place when suddenly, his eyes grew like saucers. "There are a few drawbacks," he said.

"Which are?" asked Peter.

"The only hotel suitable for the Hastings' is one owned and operated by a couple I went to high school with, and they hate me." Turning towards Peter, he added, "And the same holds true for the restaurant across the street from it."

"Oh, I see..." said Peter with his right hand touching his chin. "Warren," he confided. "Confront them and make peace. If they express liking you in front of the mayor and his wife, this town is *home free.*"

Looking dejected he said, "I tried everything, and it only gets worse."

"Warren," said Peter. "You need to try one more time. Do it for the town of Meadowdale."

Warren looked away with his arms folded in defense. After a long pause he said, "Oh, alright..."

"Good," said Peter. "The Governor's Day Celebration was a huge success. If we can get them to stay the night here and see more of the town, we'll have them in the palm of our hand."

"Then we give the gift to them?" he asked.

Peter pointed directly at Warren. "Not just *give* it to them, we'll *present it to them,*" he stressed.

"Present it to them?" asked Warren with a confused look. "How?"

Peter stood tall and addressed the mayor. *"How,* you ask? Did you forget what country you live in and *who* invented television?"

Warren was puzzled at Peter's remark. He gave a motion with his hook, signaling him to explain. A victorious expression came over the man's face as he looked up gathering his thoughts. Gracefully, his expression turned into one full of dreams as he looked off into the distance. With hands behind his back, he started to pace the floor. Peter was on the verge of expressing himself.

Warren never saw his friend behave in such a manner. Tensing up, he prepared for the worse.

"The village I came from was in awe that I made it to America," he said. "When television was invented, everyone back home wanted to know if we had one."

Warren remained calm as to not excite Peter. He nodded with understanding as his friend elaborated further.

"We couldn't afford one for years," he explained. "But the department stores had their displays with our family being one of many that often stayed there until closing time." Pivoting around he looked at Peter. "We had friends that had their own sets and sometimes they invited us over to watch television with them." Gazing up to the heavens, he said, "About that time there were a few televisions in my village, with all of my family and loved ones getting their chance to watch."

With caution, Warren studied Peter's every move and remained calm.

Peter turned towards Warren and stood at attention. "Do you know what we liked most about American television?" he asked.

"Tell me," said Warren.

Without warning Peter broke his stance and practically lunged towards the desk. Resting his hands on the polished wood, he gave the answer. "It was the game shows."

"I've always liked them," said Warren.

Peter pushed himself away from the desk and walked around the room. Looking up in a daze, he said, "We would watch Americans win prizes like a three-speed blender! Everyone in my village wanted one so that they could make milk shakes in the privacy of their own home."

"Yes, that was quite an invention," said Warren.

Peter got progressively more and more excited as his knuckles turned white. "Monte Hall would give away a box of Life Savers as a consolation prize for those who didn't have enough pennies or hairpins. Life Savers!" he proclaimed raising his index finger high in the air. "A whole box of Life Savers!"

"I like Life Savers very much," commented Warren.

Peter started to get more in-depth with his country's fascination about American game shows and focused his lone eye on the mayor. At that moment his 'wavelength' seemed to connect, with Warren starting to hear the theme song for *The Price Is Right* in his head:

Da da da daaaa Da da da daaaa da da da dada dada dada da da daaa Da da da daaa Da da da daaa...

The music progressed in volume whenever Peter would raise his voice. His erratic behavior then came within inches of the mayor's face. Staring at him point-blank, he whispered, "Do you know what?"

Warren felt endangered. He smiled back and whispered, "What?"

"We saw Tom Kennedy give away a sunshine-yellow Chevette with chocolate brown bumpers and matching interior!" Leaning back, he pounded his fist on the desk and with conviction said, "Everyone back home wished they were that contestant!" Getting his face inches from the mayor he joyfully said, "All it needed was an eight-track tape player in the dashboard." Peter's face turned into one of joy knowing Warren could envision the picture he painted.

"The women would love it," he commented.

Stepping away, he continued to pace. "My village was small and didn't realize how big America was. Many back home asked me if I personally knew Bob Barker or Monte Hall." Peter stopped and looked at his friend. "Me," he chuckled, "knowing Bob Barker and Monte Hall?"

Warren chuckled along with his friend.

Peter seemed to calm down and asked another question. "Now, Warren, how would Bill Cullen or Bob Barker present a gift to the governor?"

The music returned with eye-contact not being broken.

Daa da da daa Da da da daa Da da da dada dada dad dad da daa Da
da da daa Da da da daa Da da da dada dada dada dada dada da daa

"I don't know," responded Warren.

Smiling at his friend behind the desk, he pointed out, "They
wouldn't just *hand it to them.*"

"I guess they wouldn't," agreed Warren.

"They would have the gift behind a curtain with the whole
audience in suspense," he said. "They might even *gong* it when it
was exposed, like Chuck Barris would do."

"They just might," said Warren.

"And then the whole world would know!" shouted Peter in
triumph as he raised his hands in the air.

"Yes it would," agreed Warren.

Peter was two steps ahead of the mayor and pulled out a sheet of
paper from his pocket. Waving it in the air he said, "I will now go
to the governor's neighborhood and ask a few questions at the
local barbershop, bowling alley and cafes. I'll find out what we
need to build him a feeder that compliments him."

"Good luck," said Warren.

"Thank you," said Peter. "I'll report back to you with my
findings." The man with the eye patch left with determination.

Warren watched the door close. Taking a deep breath, he sighed,
"Wheeeew."

CHAPTER XV

T he MCC traditionally ended its classes around 3:30 PM. The dramatic increase in visitors demanded its doors stay to open past five with its art room flooded with new artists. There were just too many friendships being made to close up shop at the normal time.

The Meadowdale Retirement Home and Animal Shelter also received visitors that day. It was in recognition of the wonderful display viewed by thousands. Many checker games were played with more pets being adopted. In three days, the animal shelter's population was reduced by more than half. The ones not taken were still held numerous times and felt loved. Jayde was the *Maitre d'* greeting all who entered with many asking, "Who is Striker?"

———————

That evening had Warren Striker at home deep in thought. Wearing his bathrobe and slippers he sat on the edge of his back deck in privacy. With hook baited he again tried to tempt Maxwell within petting range. "Here, kitty, kitty, kitty. Heeerre, Maxwell—come and get your dinner," called out the bachelor. A series of kissing sounds followed with the stray just biding its time.

Warren had other things on his mind and aborted his latest attempt earlier than usual. He took the meat off of his hook and lightly tossed the tidbits near the animal. The cat walked to each piece and promptly devoured them. Next he cleaned his hands with a paper towel and picked up the high school annual he brought with him. Thumbing through the pages, he found his graduation class. The pages were wrinkled from the hundreds of times it accompanied him on lonely evenings.

Turning a page, he looked at Christine Bratton's picture. She was his high school crush: the woman he wanted to be with his entire life. Her beautiful face and wavy auburn hair with matching eyes still captivated him to this very day. Like Warren, she lived in town but hung out with her old friends; a clique that never quite accepted him.

Turning another page, his stomach started to churn as he spotted Roger Greene. Roger was *Mr. Everything.* Whether it was in the class, on the field or every party thrown by the elite, Roger was always front and center. The football hero gave Warren his first scar in life by protesting that an equipment manager wasn't worthy of a letterman Jacket. A prized jacket that mysteriously disappeared one day.

Roger went on to marry his high school sweetheart, Nancy Fields, and eventually took over his parents business: The Meadowdale Hotel. This lodge was by far the best of its kind for miles around. The situation was further complicated. The posh restaurant across the street belonged to the husband and wife team of Terry and Candice Hart. Terry was Roger's best friend since high school and never did anything without him. Candice was Christine's best friend with a few other names completing the social circle.

If the Hastings were to stay the night in Meadowdale, it would be *there.*

Turning a few more pages, he saw the face of a spirited young man with both hands folded in front of him. The name below read: *Warren Robert Striker.* A picture taken thirty pounds ago before life's acid test took over. He closed the book with a tear in his eye. *I'll just have to call them and say that I need to discuss something important over dinner,* he vowed to himself.

The next day Warren bit the bullet and personally called The Meadowdale Hotel.

"Meadowdale Hotel, Roger speaking."

"Roger, it's me, Warren Striker."

"Warren Striker?" commented Roger in a surprised tone. "What makes you call?"

Warren cut to the bone. "Look, Roger, high school was a long time ago. I realize that I'm probably your least favorite person, but I need to talk to you and your friends as soon as possible."

"This sounds important," said Roger.

"It is," said Warren. "And it's not just for me, but for the town of Meadowdale. Could you and your wife, along with Terry and his wife, meet me for dinner this week? My treat."

"Sure, we can do that, if that's what you want," answered Roger.

"Great, I appreciate that," said Warren. "Any place special you'd like to go?"

"Well, there's a Mexican place just down the street we like, if that's okay with you."

"I know which one you're talking about," said Warren. "What time works best for you?"

"Terry and Candice were coming over tonight with Christine. How about we meet you at six in the restaurant?"

"I'll be there at six," he said. "I appreciate this, Roger."

"No problem," he said. "It will do us all good to sit down together. See ya at six, Warren."

"Thanks, Roger. See ya then."

Warren wasn't sure what he was going to walk into. He concluded that it was best to simply re-introduce himself to his old rival and explain the entire situation over dinner. The rest of the day was spent doing paperwork and rehearsing what he would say in front of a mirror. Every time he began to speak, he'd stop with the confusion of not knowing what to say.

It was close to six o'clock with a nervous Warren Striker walking into the popular restaurant. He approached the hostess with Roger calling out, "Warren, over here."

Warren turned and saw Roger waving at him. He walked toward the booth where the former classmates awaited. The initial meeting was cordial with each person greeting him with sincerity. It was a natural selection for both married couples to sit together, with Warren getting to sit next to the love of his life. "Well, he said as he took the last available chair. "This is an honor."

"We're glad you're here," said Candice.

"Well, thank you," said Warren. "I'm glad to be here."

The water glasses were already full with the server arriving with an arm full of menus. "We were kicking around the idea of getting two order of their deluxe nachos and a round of ice tea," said Terry as he looked at Warren. "Does that sound good to you?"

"Sounds great to me," he replied.

Looking around the table Warren saw former classmates who were also battling the aging process. The husbands had thinning hair with a touch of gray. Their faces were developing a slight roll with their once-lean stomachs from gym class having fallen to the wayside. The wives utilized expensive outfits and makeup to hide curves and lines, with with hair dye being essential. Christine was as natural and beautiful as ever.

The server arrived with six glasses of ice tea and left. Roger wasted no time and said, "Okay, out with it Striker."

It was as good of a time as any for Warren to start his pitch. "The reason that I called you all here is that it's important that we bury the hatchet."

"What Hatchet?" asked Christine.

Roger knew what their guest was talking about. In a polite tone he requested, "Let him finish what he's trying to say."

"Thank you," replied Warren in a tactful voice. Looking down at the table he momentarily shook his head as he mustered up his courage. It was time to stand and give his presentation. Addressing the table he said, "I need you to like me for one day."

The request sounded absurd with everyone expressing a puzzled look. Terry made a comment. "Are you trying to sell us a car?"

Warren took it on the chin and looked up to the ceiling. "Ah, yes, Striker Motors..." He looked at Terry and said, "I was very proud of that business, serving the community and running television ads."

"But you were caught lying a few times and cheated some of us," said Roger.

Warren had an answer. "Are you forgetting that I was the guy who set the automotive class on fire by tossing a cigarette into a bucket of cleaning solvent?" Laughing at himself, he pointed out, "I honestly believed that my cars were fully operational. After all, I inspected them myself. When I was aware that something was wrong, I did my best to fix it. There were times I even paid a shop to do it."

Terry had something to say. "You told my dad that the Chevy you sold him was a classic and that he could get a lot of money for it. When he was driving it home, the transmission fell out of it!"

"How true," said Warren with a smile on his face. "In the meantime I had a collector call me asking if I still had the car. He offered me over twice what I sold it for. I told him of the transmission, and he still wanted it at the same price." Leaning forward, he asked a question. "Do you want to know what I did? I had him contact your father, and they made a good deal. Your dad even called me later and thanked me for selling that car to him."

Years of bottled-up frustration started to vent through Warren Striker.

Looking specifically at Roger, he said. "*I tried* when we were in high school. I tried very hard..." All eyes were on him with his intense eyes in control. "The reason I was the equipment manager was because Coach Harrison let me know that I was too small to play football." Pointing at Roger, he said, "That killed me because I wanted to be out there with you."

Roger stiffened up with a noticeable tear trickling down one eye.

"He told me that I could be just as important as the best player on the team if I would volunteer for that job, and I *believed* him. He said that all I had to do was show up early and stay an hour late. From there, I would be one of the guys at the malt shop and invited to every party. Remember the times I tried to do things with you guys after practice?" he asked. "I even talked my parents into buying me a car so that I could drive everyone places."

A sniffling could be heard as Warren continued.

"I was promised a letterman jacket if I performed that duty," he said. "It was the only way I could earn one, so I volunteered and wore it with pride."

Roger and Terry had no idea the pain Warren had gone through. They looked away as a way to avoid crying.

"I'm over that *little man complex,*" he said.

Stepping back from the table, he pointed at his shoes. "Look, I don't wear those three-inch platforms anymore!" he proclaimed. Turning around, he pointed to the back of his head."And I don't need to comb over my bald spot or dye my hair."

Warren had defended himself long enough and, with class, focused on the present situation. One that effected *everyone.*

He spoke of The Governor's Day Celebration and of the ulterior motive behind it. "The entire state is crippled, and if we can just get substantial funding..." he explained tapping his hook on the table.

"That was a wise move," commented Nancy. "You had to try something."

"I agree," said Candice.

Warren was on fire. Looking at one end of the table, he said, "We're inviting them back to stay a night in your hotel, Roger." Pointing at Terry and Candice, he added, "From there, they will have at least one meal at your restaurant. I will accompany them sharing every positive aspect I can think of about this town." With the look of a lost child he calmly said, "It makes everything better if he sees all of us like old friends."

"That's what we are!" said Roger as he left his chair giving Warren a bear hug.

The emotional moment was interrupted by a double order of deluxe nachos being served. The booth calmed down with Roger going back to his seat. Warren looked at Christine as she looked back in admiration. Reaching for a plate, he said, "Let me serve you."

CHAPTER XVI

The next morning Mayor Warren Striker was in his office when Paul Blade's voice transmitted through the intercom. "Peter Constantine is here to see you."

The message was music to Warren's ears. "Bring him in," he said. Paul opened the door, and Peter walked in carrying a large cardboard box. "We hit the jackpot!" he said, placing the box on the corner of Warren's desk. Out of breath, Peter sat down in the closest chair.

"Looks like you had success on your mission," commented the mayor.

"Big time," he replied. "Governor Hastings had a lot of friends at our celebration and they were all-too familiar with the animal feeder that was so popular. In fact, most of them had their picture taken with it!" Breathing deeply he continued. "All I had to do was stick my head into the local barbershop and explained that Meadowdale wanted to build a feeder for the governor, but needed to gather memorabilia that would best suit him. From there phone calls were made and before I knew it, I was receiving artifacts and stories left and right."

"I bet they had a lot of odds and ends," said Warren.

Peter looked at his friend with a partial look of fear. "My car bottomed-out every time I hit a bump on the way home."

"You're kidding me," said the mayor. "That much?" Peter slowly nodded with a cringe on his face.

Warren stood up and started to snap his finger trying to recall a specific word he wanted to use. "Do his interests suggest a, a, a-a-a theme? That's right, a *theme!*" he said pointing at Peter.

"We have our choice between several," said Peter. "Unless we want to blend all of them together."

"Which are?" questioned Warren.

"His hometown is well aware of his fondness for telling jokes," reported Peter as he rolled his eyes. "A local bar has an 'amateur night' once a month with Governor Hastings being known to perform on certain evenings. They donated an old stool along with a microphone on a stand."

"What else?" asked Warren.

"The man loves to golf and plays in a league. Many clubs were donated along with some balls and a metal shaft with a fluorescent flag that marked a hole."

"Good," said the mayor. "Anything else?"

"Yes there is," said Peter, "and it's something very special."

"What is it?" asked Warren.

Peter took a breath to share something that almost made him cry. Looking at his friend, he said, "James Hastings is a lot like you and me."

Warren leaned forward and rested his elbows on the desk. "What do you mean?"

"His wife, Stephanie was called to help direct us for what would be best for her husband's feeder," said Peter. "She mentioned on how he liked to play golf and make others happy with his humor, but there was something very important to him that most didn't know anything about."

"What was it?" asked Warren.

Peter got up and walked to the cardboard box. Reaching inside, he pulled out a stainless steel pet feeder that had two bowls joined together. He positioned it towards Warren with an etched inscription in plain view. The mayor looked at it and read the names *Bandit* and *Midnight*. "They are his Maxwell and Karl," said Peter in a trembling voice. "Two racoons that live in his backyard that he can't touch."

Warren slid back in his chair with eyes fixed on the metal object. "I'm not going to let you see a grown man cry," he said. The disabled man stood up, walked to the bathroom in his office, and closed the door behind him.

Peter remained quiet and stared at the treasure he was holding.

Ten minutes later Warren came out of the restroom and addressed Peter. "We need to find that boy in the picture. Let's bring everything you got to the community center. We can have that kid and his friends build Governor Hastings a feeder he will always cherish."

"I'll drive," said Peter.

It didn't take long for the mayor and his sidekick to find themselves driving down Willow Road. Soon they entered an area where patches of sawdust and grated dirt represented where homes and businesses once stood. This was the outskirts of Meadowdale, where the first tell-tale signs of an approaching recession became prevalent. "Wow," said the mayor. "They really got hit hard."

In moments, they saw a faded white structure surrounded with preschool-type images.

In shock, Warren's mouth dropped open, saying, "No, it can't be..." He scanned the overgrown grounds noticing the absence of other buildings that once stood there. Looking at Peter, he said, "When I was a kid, this was where the rich people lived." They entered the parking lot only to be further confused. Almost every parking space was taken with two buses near the front entrance. "What's going on here?" he questioned out loud.

"Let's get a parking space and go inside," suggested Peter.

Peter parked the car and walked with Warren into the MCC. The homemade artwork that covered the walls and fences continued inside. The two were now in the lobby that surrounded them with multicolored walls that adorned murals and framed artwork. There was *life* projected here with an undeniable aura of pride. What this run-down building of yesterday lacked in financial backing, it made up for in spirit!

"Look over here," said Peter. Warren stood next to Peter and saw that someone had cut Chase's picture out of the newspaper and framed it.

A voice grabbed their attention. "Mayor Striker and Mr. Constantine, it's great to have you two here." Turning around they saw Andy Rutledge in his wheelchair. "Can I assist you in any way?

Handshakes were exchanged with brief introductions.

"Call me Peter."

"Call me Warren."

"I'm Andy."

"We're looking for Chase Mansfield," said Mayor Striker. "As mayor of this town, I want to congratulate him on his achievement and shake his hand."

"We're all proud of him," said Andy. "I'm sure he'll be honored to meet you."

"There was something that we were going to ask of him," said Warren.

"What?" asked Andy.

"Our governor and his wife were most impressed with that cute spaceman he built that feeds pets," explained the mayor. "It has come to our attention that Governor Hastings has a special place in his heart for all animals. His wife and friends assembled various items that represent his interests. This was in hopes that Chase and his friends could construct him a 'personal' pet feeder as a surprise gift."

Andy looked at the two visitors and with a smile said, "I think they would be more than happy to do that. How about introducing yourself to everyone in our homeroom and personally ask Chase? He'd like that."

Peter and Warren looked at each other shaking their heads. Looking at Andy, Warren said, "We'd love that."

"Follow me," said Andy as he turned around and wheeled down the hallway. Once entering the room it came to an abrupt silence. The two most photographed men in the Meadowdale Gazette were gracing their presence. "We have some special visitors that would like to talk to us for a moment," announced Andy. The many present immediately gave an ovation.

Warren stood up in front of the MCC with Peter at his side. He thanked them for their kindness and praised them for winning all of the awards at The Governor's Day Celebration. Then he got down to business.

Holding everyone's attention, Mayor Warren Striker pointed his renowned silver hook at Chase Mansfield and said, "Chase, the reason we're here is because the town of Meadowdale needs you."

"That's right," commented the popular man with one eye. The fifteen-year-old had never felt so *important* in his entire life and sat up at attention.

Mayor Warren Striker continued. He talked about how their display was considered to be the best that anyone has ever seen. Next he pointed out how deep the line was for those who wanted their picture taken with *Sparkles*. Peter displayed his cell phone picture to the room.

Warren elaborated about the beauty of the feeder and how it could feed any animal, while making all who saw it fall in love with it. Eventually, he mentioned Governor Hastings and his wife, and how they left Meadowdale *wanting one.*

"The governor's wife and their friends gave us lots of things that could be used to build his feeder," said the mayor.

Warren made his move.

"Chase, do you think you and your friends could build Governor Hastings a feeder that will always make him happy?"

If anyone questions how a spirited group from the MCC could take on this task, then look up the name Franklin D. Roosevelt. He was the 32nd president of the United States of America who led his country out of the Great Depression with his theme song, *Happy Days Are here Again.* When diagnosed with polio and confined to a wheelchair, he merely applied it to help others by forming *The March Of Dimes.* A non-profit organization created to enhance health for all mothers and babies.

If one wishes to be more current, then names like Peter Longstaff, Alice Schoenfield and Lisa Fittipaldi could serve as further testimony. Each is an artist who overcame deficiencies that ranged from having no arms to being legally blind.

Their contribution to life?

Artwork that serves as a universal language that greatly inspires all who see. A creativity that encourages the world to realize that *no one* is prohibited from having a great achievement.

How could anyone even question if Chase Mansfield and his friends could accomplish this momentous task?

And Now:

Back to our story.

All eyes were on Chase Mansfield. His answer would be one that showed the faith he had in the MCC and its ever-increasing membership. "We can do it," he said with authority. Mayor Warren

Striker raised his hand and hook in victory as the whole room erupted in cheer.

Chase Mansfield just made a decision that would forever change the course of Meadowdale, with the world taking notice.

CHAPTER XVII

S teve, along with his son, Allen and John Mansfield transported the artifacts from Peter Constantine's car into the art room. They were now sizing up what they had to work with and what could be made.

Steve Smith worked intently spreading out the many golf clubs, microphones and pet feeders donated for the new MCC project. The graduate from Casper, Wyoming's Certified Welding and Trade School would again use his expertise to assist Chase on this most-important project. His connections with those he worked with would allow *anything* to get chrome plated.

It was now time to play *scrabble* and draw their ideas on paper.

"How about we do something like this," said Allen. He sketched a series of golf clubs and placed them end-to-end, making a pyramid type structure out of it."

"Well," said his dad looking at it from different angles. "That's an idea."

John started to doodle and drew three microphone stands as legs to hold up a golf bag. "Da-daaa," he sang out waving his hands frantically like a magician.

"Not, bad," said Allen.

Steve made his attempt by illustrating golf clubs to cage-in a comic's chair. "Whaddya guys think?" he asked.

"Hmmm, his wife will like it on the nights she's upset with him," commented John.

Chase arrived and by looking at the table and sketches, knew what they were doing. "Can I try?" he asked.

"Be our guest," said Allen.

Chase walked around the table and studied the material that lay on it. Methodically he walked around the room and glanced at a picture of a peacock. A grin came over his face understanding the idea that popped into his head. The boy leaned over a nearby table and began to draw a design.

Steve, Allen and John quietly watched.

In a few minutes Chase was done and presented his idea, causing three jaws to drop with mouths wide open. What they saw clearly illustrated how Chase Mansfield's genius understood others.

Chase hit the bullseye. "We need to select the pieces we'll be using and have everyone make sure that they are spotless," said Steve. "After that, I'll take the parts to a local foundry and get them chromed. Then I'll weld it together. Once that's done, we will involve everyone to polish it." He looked at Chase and – giving a thumbs-up – said, "It will be immaculate when we're finished."

Andy Rutledge was leaning back quietly, laughing for joy. When the materials arrived, he secretively hid, waiting to see what Chase would dream up...

———————

That week a dedicated MCC was working in full force. Two days were devoted to cleaning off the metal pieces that would soon be transferred to a local foundry. Buckets of soapy water, scouring pads and elbow grease served as the tools necessary to perform. Work shirts that were provided became damp and soiled with no one complaining.

Finally, the cleansed material was off campus and being bathed in an industrial-sized vat. When the treated metal arrived back home, Steve carefully inspected Chases blueprints and began to weld.

Once assembled, every hand in the MCC help polished the makeshift feeder until it reflected like a mirror.

Steve called Mayor Striker and requested that Peter and the governor's wife visit the MCC and critique the new feeder. "I can't wait to see it," replied Warren Striker. The man with the hook made two phone calls and left his office. Just before closing time Warren, Peter and Stephanie were in the art room gazing at the shimmering conglomeration of modern art.

"It's beautiful!" said Stephanie. "He'll love it. It captures everything!"

"Th-th-they made that?" uttered Peter in amazement.

Warren gave a long whistle. "It says *Meadowdale* all over it!" he exclaimed.

What they saw was a comic's stool with golf clubs spread behind it like a peacock's feathers. In front were two golf clubs that protruded from both sides of the stool, inches off the ground. They joined together a foot in front of the stool with a microphone on a stand that rested on the front point where the clubs met. From there it angled upward a few feet above the stool, ready for a show.

The stainless steel bowls that displayed the names *Bandit* and *Midnight* were attached just below where the stand met the clubs—like a footrest on a barbershop chair. The icing on the cake was a pole on the very back, dead center. It was fastened where all of the *peacock feathers* met and stood several feet above the rest displaying its bright triangular flag.

At one angle, it *did* resemble a bumper car that received its power from a suspended mesh screen conducting electricity. Another view suggested that it might be a barber's chair. From another position, it was more like a golf cart, but to squint and look sideways, one could see a stage ready for a comic to perform.

"Who designed this?" asked Peter.

"I'll give you one guess," replied Steve.

"Was it that boy who won those awards with that spaceman-looking animal feeder?" asked Stephanie.

After the viewing Warren, Peter and Stephanie agreed to have an early dinner at a nearby Thai restaurant. Sitting at their table Stephanie made another comment. "I can't believe what they have done for James."

Peter inconspicuously kicked Warren's leg under the table and got his attention. The man with an eye patch made a 'surging facial expression' without Stephanie being aware. Warren understood that he was being cued to discuss bringing the governor and his wife back to Meadowdale for a more-in-depth visit.

"Stephanie," said the mayor. "This town loves your husband and feels blessed having him as our governor. "We are inviting the two of you to pick a time when you can stay the night in our finest hotel, have dinner on us and then we will surprise him with his new feeder."

"Oh, he would just love that!" said Stephanie Hastings. "We have a daughter that is a freelance writer. She missed out on the Governor's Day Celebration and wished that she could have been there to write an article about it. Do you mind if we bring her along so that she can take pictures and publish a story about this?

Warren looked at Peter. *This* was what they were hoping for. Looking at Stephanie, he spoke in an accommodating tone. "By all means, we'd love to have her. Let me know when the three of you are ready, and we'll set things up."

"I'll call you tomorrow morning," she said with enthusiasm.

Warren Striker drove home after having one of the best days in his life. The MCC proved that people just like *him* do count and are appreciated. *I wish they were there for me when I was growing up...* he thought to himself.

He also found the trump card needed to boost the town he represented by addressing the governor a second time on a more personal level. A tactic, if performed right, would be well publicized through the journalism of Governor Hasting's daughter.

His day of enlightenment would continue to *roll sevens.* Pulling into his driveway, he noticed a beautifully wrapped present with a card tucked underneath some ribbon. He anxiously left his car and walked to his porch. Picking up the present, he looked up and then down the street to see if anyone was watching him. There was no one around. With keys in hand, he quickly entered his home and sat down with the package.

He opened the card and read it.

Warren, you were great at dinner the other night, but I only know you as being great. This gift was something that I only recently found out about. I will call you for coffee this week. Please wear it when we meet!

Love, Christine

The former equipment manager put the card down and held the present with both hands. He inspected the conservative wrapping of white paper with diagonal silver and black lines. Classic red ribbon with a matching bow made the gift almost too beautiful to open. But *that* wouldn't stop him.

With caution, he removed the bow, ribbons and unwrapped the box as to not tear any paper. Once the white rectangle box was exposed, he removed the cover. Looking at him was a mint-condition red, white and blue Meadowdale Patriots letterman jacket with his name, *Warren* stitched in red on the traditional left-hand side.

At that moment his telephone rang...

CHAPTER XVIII

C hase Mansfield was enjoying dinner with his mother and uncle. "Mom," he asked. "Do you think Governor Hasting will let a lot of animals eat out of his feeder?"

"Why, yes," answered Julia. "It's just like the one you built for Humphrey. Every creature that God created knows that Humphrey is their friend, and that they can always go to 'Sparkles' whenever they get hungry."

Chase displayed an expression of relief as he looked up thinking of the many pets that would never again go hungry. "God wanted you to make sure that no animal would ever go hungry again," injected his uncle, John.

"Can we build more feeders for others?" asked Chase.

"Sure," replied his uncle. "What the MCC has made is something that *anyone* would want."

"And it's all because of you," said his mother.

———————

Striker Headquarters the following morning:

Mayor Warren Striker was just on the phone with Stephanie Hastings. It was agreed the couple would check in at the Meadowdale Hotel that Friday evening at six o-clock and meet Warren and Peter for dinner across the street at seven. In the meantime, Stephanie personally arranged for her daughter,

Shaffon, to drop by Mayor Striker's office around noon that day and introduce herself.

The call ended with each thanking the other for their cooperation. "This is going to be so much fun!" said Stephanie. "See you and Peter this Friday at seven."

"I agree and can hardly wait," said Warren. "We'll be there." He hung up the phone and promptly called his friend, Peter Constantine.

Within one ring Peter answered saying, "Tell me everything, Warren."

Warren let Peter know that everything was going according to plan. He explained that the governor's daughter would be dropping by at noon to introduce herself and ask a few questions. "I'd like you to be here," requested Warren.

"You can count on me," came Peter's reply.

Warren and Peter were conversing about sports and classic cars when Paul Blade's voice called out through the intercom. "There is a Shaffon Hastings here to see you, Mayor Striker."

Warren leaned over the speaker box and pressed the button that would allow him to be heard. "Please send her in," he said. The two men turned to the office door and with anticipation watched it open. The woman who came into view was what they would expect from a governor's daughter. She was breathtaking, and possessed her mother's image. From the shoulder-length blonde hair and blue eyes to her distinct look and conservative dress, she was intoxicating.

Warren walked up to the twenty-eight-year-old and introduced himself. "Shaffon, this is such an honor to meet you. I'm Warren Striker." He extended his good hand and gently shook her hand.

"I've heard and read so much about you," said the freelance writer with her charm. "And my parents think the world about you. It's great to meet you, Mayor Striker."

"Call me Warren," he said playfully.

"I like that," she said with a giggle. "Pleased to meet you, Warren."

Directing his hook towards Peter, he made a second introduction. "If you know who I am, then you must have heard about Peter Constantine."

"Peter Constantine?" questioned Shaffon as she laughed to herself. "You mean that great man who is always donating his time to worthwhile causes? This entire area knows who he is." Extending her hand, she introduced herself, "Pleased to meet you, Peter."

"The pleasure is mine," replied Peter.

"Would you like some coffee or tea?" asked Warren.

"Coffee sounds good," replied Shaffon.

"Make it two," said Peter.

"I'll make it three," said Warren. He leaned over his desk and spoke through the intercom. "Paul, would you mine brewing a fresh pot of coffee and put it into a thermos? When it's done, I'd appreciate it if you would bring it here. We'll also need three cups with some cream and sugar."

"I'll get on it right now," replied the loyal aide.

Peter's etiquette addressed their guest. "Please, let me hang your coat for you."

"Thank you," said Shaffon.

In minutes, they were all seated at a table with coffee cups in hand. "Your mother told me you are a freelance writer," commented Warren.

"That's why I'm here," she replied. "My parents told me of the great time they had at the Governor's Day Celebration. I was out of town on an assignment and wished I was here to cover that story." Taking a sip of coffee, she continued. "This morning I was at the Meadowdale Community Center and met the boy who was in the paper. I interviewed him and had him pose for a few pictures with the feeders. Chase certainly is a nice boy, and so are the people who are involved with the center. They're so spirited!" she added.

Warren and Peter nodded.

"Do you mind if I ask a few questions?" asked the reporter.

"Not at all," replied the mayor.

Shaffon got out her notepad and prepared to write. "It seems that this town might be known for starting a new trend," she stated. "Do you have a specific name for those pet feeders I took pictures of this morning?"

"Why, yes we do," answered Warren.

"Good," said Shaffon as she intently held a pen. "What are they referred to as?"

Warren looked like a kid in grade school lying about his homework. Scratching his head with his hook he looked up rolling his eyes. "Now let me think. It's called a-a..."

The mayor needed help as he looked at Peter. The man with a slight accent took a 'shot in the dark' and blurted out, "We call them a *Meadowdale Feeder*.

Warren Striker slapped his hand on his lap and said, "That's right, they're called *Meadowdale Feeders*.

Shaffon was greatly amused with their teamwork and wrote down the product's name.

"Next question," she said. "How does one get a Meadowdale Feeder?"

Peter came to the mayor's aid. Shrugging his shoulders and exposing the palms of his hands, he gave the answer. "To get a Meadowdale Feeder, one would have to come to Meadowdale."

"Good answer," commented Shaffon as she wrote down the information. "This next one is meant for the mayor of

Meadowdale." Leaning back in her chair, she asked. "Are you saying that you sell the customer a package to come to your town and get their feeder?"

Warren gave a direct answer. "Yes."

"Wonderful," said Shaffon. "Tell me all about it."

Warren took a sip of coffee and placed his mug on the table. He formally stood up and began pacing behind his chair. Mayor Warren Striker was in the spotlight and cleared his throat.

"What the town of Meadowdale is offering- is a fun-filled *getaway* where the customer takes in the many good things on which this town prides itself. They will be staying at our finest hotel with first-class service. From there, our restaurants, pizza parlors, shops, parks and people will make the stay well worthwhile."

Warren stopped and pointed his shiny hook at Shaffon. "Then the fun starts," he said with a clever grin. "The recipient has no idea what they're walking into, but their loved ones do. After all, they are the ones who supplied the community center with the artifacts needed to build that special, unique, one-of-a-kind Meadowdale Feeder that's waiting to be claimed. Once that customer sees the feeder that was specially crafted just for them, they will deem it as a priceless heirloom."

Warren raised his hook in the air. "That's because it came from their own past and was created out of love from those lonely and disadvantaged citizens that call that place *home.*" Warren leaned inches away from Shaffon's face and quietly said, "Just like the one you just saw waiting for your father."

Standing straight up and pacing the room, Warren projected his voice as he raised his hook. "As mayor of Meadowdale, I can guarantee that those who pay to have this *Meadowdale Experience* will always want to come back."

In tears, Shaffon dropped her pad and pen. On impulse, she ran to the mayor, hugging him. Peter was taken by the moment and took out a handkerchief from his jacket. He covered his face with it, turned to his side and balled his eyes out.

"Is that what you call this?" asked Shaffon sniffling. "The Meadowdale Experience?"

Warren looked up while patting the sobbing woman on the back. He thought for a moment and liked the name. "That's right," he said with confidence. "We call our package, "The Meadowdale Experience."

Peter recovered and stood up clapping his hands. "Bravo, bravo!" he cheered. "The Meadowdale Experience will be an adventure everyone would want to try!"

Shaffon regained her composure and returned to her chair. "Wow," she commented. "This will be fun!"

"It will," said Warren. "Be sure to be with your parents throughout this *experience*."

Shaffon was already committed. "I'll be with them from the time we check into the hotel until the time dad takes his feeder home." The woman looked at her watch and said, "I'm due back at the office."

Peter got her coat and helped her put it on. "I love what's going on in this town," she said. "I'll write an article full of pictures that cover The Meadowdale Experience."

"We appreciate that," said Warren. "Please call me when you get checked-in this Friday. Peter and I will be taking you and your family out to dinner."

"I'm looking forward to it," said Shaffon.

The woman who arrived with handshakes left with hugs.

Warren walked behind his desk and sat down. Looking at his friend he said, "Things are shaping up."

"They certainly are," agreed Peter. "Did you make amends with your old classmates that run the hotel and restaurant?"

Warren clasped his hook and hand behind his head and said, "Well, there's one I know of who doesn't hate me, but I still don't know about the others."

"Well," said Peter. "That's a start."

"I've got to make a lot of calls now," said Warren. "First, I have to confirm reservations for the hotel and dinner. Then I need to contact the MCC and come up with a flashy way to present the governor's feeder with the right touch.

Peter's face lost all expression as he focused on the mayor. Standing up, he questioned, "Did I hear you right? Flashy? *The right touch?*"

Warren leaned as far back as his chair would allow as Peter firmly placed two fists on his desk. "Don't you watch cable at one o'clock in the morning?" he scolded. "They're all there!" he exclaimed. "Bob Barker, Monty Hall, Tom Kennedy. They're all there..."

The theme song to *The Price is Right* entered Warren's head at a low setting. The volume immediately increased as the obsessed game show viewer went into further detail.

Da da da daa Da da da daa Da da da dada dada dada dada da daa
Da da da daa Da da da daa Da da da dada dada dada dada da daa

"They never hesitated with their perfect timing," the naturalized citizen pointed out.

Warren looked at his naked wrist and said, "Oh, I'm running late for an appointment."

"Were the contestants ever late when they had an opportunity to take home a Ron Popeil's Veg-O-Matic?" he asked with a smirk on his face.

Staring at the hairs on his wrist, Warren again attempted to change subjects. "I better run, this is an important meeting." Without looking at Peter, he ran for his safety, grabbing his hat and coat. "Be sure to lock up when you leave," he yelled charging out the door.

CHAPTER XIX

Warren arrived at the MCC and held a small conference. "We only have a few days to come up with some clever way to present the governor his feeder," he explained. Looking off at a distance he said, "Peter had an idea, but I just don't know..."

"What was his thought?" asked John Mansfield.

Warren took a deep breath and started to explain. "Do you remember those game shows we saw on TV when we were kids? He wants to set up a production where the present is behind a curtain with everyone in suspense. He even considered having a gong sound when the present was exposed to the contestant and audience."

"That sounds like fun!" said Julia.

"We have an auditorium where we can do that right here," said Steve.

"It will be like a play," said Renée "Everyone will have a part and really get into it!"

"Warren," said Andy. "You have a lot on your plate addressing the formalities having the Governor and his family stay here. How about letting then MCC take care of the presentation? When you and the Hastings arrive, everything will be ready. Trust us."

"That would be a great help," said the mayor. "Can we schedule this for, about...two o'clock this Saturday afternoon?"

"I promise we'll be ready at that time," said Renée."

"This is going to be a blast!" exclaimed John.

Warren looked around at the table and said, "Okay, we'll be here this Saturday at two."

The mayor left with the MCC uniting and discussing a plan.

Next, Mayor Warren Striker would have to go behind enemy lines a second time and contact Roger Greene and Terry Hart.

"Meadowdale Hotel, Roger speaking."

"Roger, it's me. Warren Striker."

"Warren!" addressed a jubilant Roger Greene. "How are you doing today?"

"Well, I think I'm doing okay," said Warren. "I called to make reservations for the governor and his family for this Friday. It will be for a party of three, and they will check in around six in the afternoon."

"Just one moment," said Roger. "There, all taken care of. That was great going out with you the other night. Everyone loved seeing you and wants to do it again."

"I appreciate that," said Warren. "It was a good evening for me too. I have to call Terry now and make dinner reservations for seven o'clock."

"Dinner for how many?" asked Roger.

"There will be five of us," answered Warren.

"Let me take care of the dinner reservations," said Roger. "We'll have our best room waiting for the governor and his family, and you'll have reservations for five across the street an hour later."

"Thanks, Roger. I appreciate you handling things for me," said Warren.

"No problem, Warren; you're worth it. Just drop by and say, "Hi" to me when you get here."

"I'll do more than that," said Warren. "See ya Friday."

The mayor was tying up all loose ends. Next he would call Stephanie Hastings to update their progress. "You might want to call the MCC just to see if they wanted to inform you about anything," suggested the mayor.

"That's a good idea," said Stephanie.

Warren dictated the ten-digit number to her and finished by saying, "Everything's a go! I'll see you, your husband, and that wonderful daughter of yours this Friday at seven for dinner. It will be at the restaurant across the street from where you are staying."

"We'll be there," said Stephanie. "And, thank you so-much, Warren."

"*You* are very welcome," came the reply.

The mayor hung up the phone. Looking up an unexpected presence startled him. There before him was Christine standing with her hands on her waist doing her imitation of an upset mother. "Are you so busy that you forgot about meeting me across the street for coffee?"

Warren couldn't believe that he forgot about their engagement. "Chris, I was on the run all day and it completely slipped my mind!"

Christine was well aware on how busy Warren was. Recently, he was 'the talk of the town' with everybody viewing him more favorably. "Looks like you could use a break," she said. "But first, where's that jacket you promised to wear?"

"I didn't forget it," he said walking to the closet. "I got here this morning looking forward to being with you, then everything seemed to happen all at once." He took the letterman jacket off the hanger and said, "There's just one problem." Putting on the decorative garment, it appeared to be three sizes too small. "I wished I stayed in shape the way my jacket did," he said patting his stomach.

"You look fine," she said.

"Here," he said taking it off. "Let's see how it looks on you."

Warren helped Christine into the award jacket and stood back. With arms extended he positioned his hands like a photographer focusing on a subject. It fit perfectly with Christine looking proud. "You look beautiful," he said. "I want you to keep it."

The woman put her arms around the man, kissing him on the cheek. "This is the best gift I ever had," she said. "And now, I'm taking you out for dinner."

Warren Robert Striker just had a dream come true: He was mayor of the town he grew up in with Christine at his side, wearing his jacket...

Friday evening arrived with Mayor Warren Striker and Peter Constantine entering the town's most premier restaurant: Hart's Diner. The two dignitaries were dressed semi-formal as they entered the five-star restaurant. Warren had knots in his stomach. He recently saw the good side of the high school clique that use to ridicule him at every chance. He credited their last meeting as being productive, but did it *really* change things?

Warren Striker pondered over the endless possibilities:

Would there be another bucket of water over a door jamb waiting for the shortest boy in school?

Would there be a 'play-on-words' that utilized a code meant to degrade him further?

Would they gather around him just to make sure that everyone would see that he was not allowed to be part of their conversation?

Walking up to the hostess, the controversial mayor heard his name called out. "Warren!" Turning, he saw Terry and Roger. They were walking towards them with polished teeth and extended hands.

From the corner of his eye, he saw the Hastings watch as Shaffon took notes.

Roger reached his hand behind Warren's back and shook with the other. "It's great to see you, guy—you look great!" Immediately, Roger's class continued. The hotel owner extended a hand to Peter and introduced himself. "My name is Roger Greene."

Peter loved the reception and clasped his hand. "Peter Constantine at your service," he said with a wink.

Terry followed suit with the governor and his family most impressed.

"Your guest just got here," stated Terry.

At that moment, the governor placed his hand on Warren's shoulder getting his attention. "You certainly have a lot of friends around here. When we arrived at the hotel and mentioned that we were here to see you, they insisted that we stay for free."

Shaffon grinned in approval as she continued to write more notes.

Graciously, Terry led the party to the 'Captain's Table'; the best seats in the house. Once seated, Warren's gift of gab kept a rotation of laughter with everyone getting equal time.

The meal was incredible from seafood appetizers to flaming desserts. The highlight came at the end when Terry Hart himself addressed the group. The successful entrepreneur placed his hands behind his back and matched the honor Roger's hotel gave. "Now I don't want any trouble," said Terry. "Any friend of Warren is family to us. As proprietor of Hart's Diner we'd like to welcome Governor Hastings and his family back to Meadowdale and hope that we have the honor of serving you again. We insist that this meal is on us and thank you."

Shaffon asked Terry if she could take a few pictures of him and the staff. "We'd love that!" he said.

The old high school gang had made their amends to Warren. The classmate who was always denied was vindicated at a most crucial time. With full stomachs and wind in their sails, the Meadowdale nightlife awaited. A walk through the Town Square Park with its trees, plants and fountains would give ample time to further visit. After that, a few local antique shops would still be open to wind down the evening.

It was getting late with the Hastings being escorted to the Meadowdale Hotel. They expressed gratitude for a great evening. It was agreed that Warren and Peter would pick them up at 1:30 the next afternoon to visit the Meadowdale Community Center before returning home. Upon leaving the hotel, Stephanie got Warren and Peter's attention by clearing her throat. When they turned towards her, she gave a wink and made an 'okay' sign with her hand.

CHAPTER XX

D-Day had arrived with Warren and Peter picking up the Hastings.

"Did you enjoy your stay at the hotel?" asked the mayor.

"They treated us like royalty," said Governor Hastings.

"We had breakfast across the street with everyone mentioning the great job you do for this town," said Stephanie.

"Well," said Warren. "Our community center wanted to give you a send-off. "Who am I to argue?" he commented in an agreeable tone.

Shaffon was busy taking down notes.

Mayor Striker asked, "Are you checked out yet?"

"Yes," said James. "Our luggage is already in our car."

"Okay," said Warren. "I'll drive to the Meadowdale Community Center and you can follow me."

Everything was going according to plan. Warren Striker was again feeling the anxiety of not knowing *exactly* what lay ahead at the MCC.

"Do you think they're ready?" he asked Peter.

"They will be ready by their standards," he replied.

They entered the parking lot to see it practically full. Driving by the main entrance was a well-marked reserved parking space. The sign read:

Reserved For Governor Hastings.

James Hastings tooted his horn acknowledging that he saw his space.

Within minutes, the party of five were entering the doors of the MCC with Andy Rutledge there to greet them.

"James, it's good to see you again," said the man in the wheelchair.

"I remember you, Andy," came the hospitable reply.

"Well," said Andy. "Since everyone has been introduced, we might as well get seated." He turned his chair around and led the way to the auditorium. Butterflies mounted in Warren's stomach. This main event would take place in a public hall from another era. A place that he never laid eyes on before. The mayor thought to himself: *Would this once popular meeting place for shows and conventions be in any condition for such a grand occasion?*

With crossed fingers, he held his breath and entered the MCC auditorium. Again, he was more than just pleasantly surprised. What they found was a preserved theater with a lobby serving beverages and desserts. It was the same forum where the elite once conducted their many socials. Thoughtfully, it had been set aside and mothballed.

There was more.

Many of the governor's friends, family and colleagues were waiting for James Hastings to arrive and surrounded him. The entire Meadowdale City Council and media was also there. The governor was shocked.

A relieved Warren Striker looked around to see who he should thank. Along the far wall was Andy, Renée, Julia, John and Steve. They got his attention and together, gave a reassuring thumbs up. Looking back, he saluted his hook.

Pats on the back with handshakes and introductions were followed by stories and side-splitting laughter.

Soon Renée Klause projected her voice and announced that it was time for everyone to get a seat. She introduced herself to Governor Hastings and led the group to the honor section: front row and center seats. The auditorium was over half full with the Meadowdale High School Band sitting off to the side.

It was the moment of truth.

Everything Mayor Striker, Peter Constantine, the MCC, and the entire community worked for was on the line.

This was the grand finale, and it represented a matrix that had many facets. One that was impossible to do alone, involving many unsung heroes. Throughout this journey, there were those of questionable character and ability that simply had to be trusted, causing undue stress for the politician with one hook. Until now, everything worked out surprisingly well. Still, the most important element was about to take place with everything blind to one Warren Striker.

Sitting between Peter and the governor, he began to wonder...

What does the MCC have up its sleeve?

Would their presentation be a hit, or would it merely be a reflection of the town's disadvantage being on the lowest budget allowed?

Would Governor Hastings like his Meadowdale Feeder, or would it be regarded as a tasteless piece of junk?

It was now time for the final show. The finishing touch that would decide if their strategy to draw attention to Meadowdale and boost the local economy would work.

Renée took stage with Andy. Dolly joined in wearing welcome signs for the governor and his family. Renée started off by welcoming everyone to the MCC and explaining that a short play was about to be performed.

Andy took over by mentioning that Renée would then sing two Mamas and Papas songs and *stressed* that they would love it.

Renée continued stating that the MCC was representing the town of Meadowdale and would finish up their performance with a surprise package for the governor.

The play began with every MCC member having a part. It was written by Renée herself and was called *Neighborly Prayers.*

It was about a place where everyone lived alone and tried to grow their own food. Every time someone tried to grow a crop, they were missing something needed to do so. Eventually, each person would pray to God and ask who to borrow from. When they had a prayer answered, they were all too happy to lend.

Finally, people started to exchange their produce with others in order to get a variety. From there, they established a town where everyone prayed, worked together and lived in harmony.

The town created was named *Meadowdale.* Everyone in the audience gave a standing ovation.

Renée followed with the backing of the Meadowdale High School band. She sang, *Dream a Little Dream of Me* and *Words of Love.* The place went crazy!

Once Renée got off stage the lights were turned off with several spotlights panning the audience aimlessly. Instantly the high school band began to play the theme song for *The Price Is Right.*

Da da da daa Da da da daa Da da da dada dada dada dada dada da daa Da da da daa Da da da daa Da da da dada dada dada dada dada da daa

Warren was caught off-guard and almost jumped out of his chair. Looking at Peter, he saw what resembled a child on Christmas morning. The man with one eye had a delirious look on his face that telegraphed: *I want more.*

A lone spotlight stood still on Governor Hastings with the clairvoyant voice of Steve Smith calling out:

"Governor James Hastings, come ooonn down!"

John and Julia Mansfield popped up out of nowhere and escorted the governor on stage. The lights came on with James Hastings facing Steve Smith. Steve dressed in a black ceremonial tuxedo with tails and stovepipe hat. He was obviously playing the role of a game show host and held an antique megaphone used for cheerleading.

The music stopped.

"Governor Hastings, welcome to Meadowdale!" said Steve as the entire audience clapped.

"Well, it's nice to be here," he responded.

Steve was widely known for his fun personality and held everyone at the edge of their seat. He mentioned on how much the town appreciated him as a governor who always looked after everyone. The Governor's Day celebration was mentioned with cheers being heard. Steve asked him if he remembered the funny looking Martian-type feeder that won two ribbons.

"Remember it?" asked the Governor. "My wife and I would like to get one."

Those words played right into Steve's presentation. Using the megaphone, he aimed towards the crowd. "And if you get one, do you solemnly swear to love, honor and feed it until death do you part?" The crowd laughed.

James was a good sport. He intentionally overly-reacted by clasping his hands together and getting down on one knee. "I promise!"

Steve raised the megaphone to his mouth and asked, "How about for in sickness and health?"

"I do, I do!" cried out the official. People were howling.

Steve continued with the vows. "What about for richer or poor?"

"Anything!" pleaded Governor Hastings.

Steve put the megaphone on the floor and pulled out a scroll tucked inside his jacket. Rolling it open with both hands he read:

"Governor James Hastings you are now the proud father of a sixty-three-pound, four-ounce, Meadowdale Feeder!"

At that moment, Chase Mansfield entered the stage from the far right holding a sledgehammer. Everyone was watching, not knowing what to expect.

He walked up to an easel that was off to the side, a configuration that went by unnoticed. The metal tripod matched his height and was secured to the floor. Welded to the iron frame was a thin sheet of metal the size of a door. A flattened trash can lid was bolted dead center. The crumbled disc was painted like a bullseye used for archery. It was outlined in red, with an inner red circle and a six-inch red dot in the center. He positioned himself like a baseball player at bat and clobbered it. The noise startled everyone and could be heard outside the building.

Bwaaamm!

The curtain behind the stage opened with the band playing Warren Striker's favorite song once again: The theme song to *The Price Is Right.*

Da da da daa Da da da daa Da da da dada dada dada dada dada da daa Da da dad daa Da da da daa Da da da dada dada dada dada dada da daa

Those watching were flabbergasted from what stood before them. The remainder of the MCC stood in the background like a choir ready to perform. Each wore their bright MCC shirt that had their name printed on it. In front of them was James Hasting's golf team posing in a tight formation. Closer was his wife and daughter who got back stage undetected when he was pulled from the audience.

Front and center was the grand prize. The showpiece those on stage bowed down to. It was a glistening, chrome plated Meadowdale Feeder created specifically for James Hastings. A one-of-a-kind masterpiece that commemorated two residences that shared his back yard: Bandit and Midnight.

The band stopped playing with the room silenced. Governor Hastings walked up to the polished feeder and then looked back at the friends and family scattered about in the audience. He turned around and looked at his beautiful wife and daughter, and then at his golfing buddies.

Next he studied every face in the back row, knowing that they all sacrificed to present this special gift to him. Looking around in a turning motion, he said, "You did all of this for me?"

The room erupted into a standing ovation that brought tears to the Hastings family. "It's beautiful!" he exclaimed circling his present. His wife and daughter walked up to him and hugged with the golf team and MCC members surrounding him. Soon the entire assembly swarmed the stage to be with James Hastings, his family, golf buddies and meet the members of the MCC. They would also get a closer look at the latest Meadowdale Feeder.

Chase was recognized by the governor. James approached the boy who created the first Meadowdale Feeder and asked, "Did you make this happen?"

"We all did," replied Chase. Out of innocence, the boy asked a question that would cause many to pay a price. "Hey, don't you like to tell jokes?"

Governor Hastings loved what he heard. He saw Renée and requested that everyone get back in their seats. She gave the announcement with the request being fulfilled.

Without warning, James Hastings sat down in the comic's stool that centered his feeder and addressed his audience. It was too late for those present to avoid what was about to happen.

"A funny thing happened to me on the way..."

CHAPTER XXI

$\int$ unday morning had the entire town of Meadowdale spend extra time at their breakfast table.

Q. The reason?

A. The Meadowdale Gazette and its affiliates published a full page article written by one Shaffon Hastings entitled:

The Meadowdale Experience

Have You Ordered Your Meadowdale Feeder Yet?

The article was more of a pictorial that captured Governor Hastings and his family partaking in the inaugural *Meadowdale Experience* package. It documented their journey through the town of Meadowdale, from their arrival at the hotel to the informal 'game show of yesterday' at the community center. The featured article accounted for all of the fun and excitement they encountered every step of the way.

Most important, the governor's personal Meadowdale Feeder was pictured. It was explained that each participant would have their own, one-of-a-kind feeder waiting at the end of their journey. A prized Meadowdale Feeder based on what their loved ones supplied for materials.

This front page story also served a justice. It started off with the picture of Chase Mansfield that initially made the paper weeks earlier. It finished with him posing with Sparkles and the governor's feeder. His cause for wanting to feed *animals everywhere* was clearly stated.

Throughout the state and beyond, family vacations were being planned with attics and garages being rummaged through. Trinkets and memorabilia of yesterday's glory would now be enshrined forever at the very community center where Chase Mansfield worked. Dad's retirement, sister's graduation, Grandma's 90th along with other milestones would be honored through *The Meadowdale Experience.*

The newsprint finished by giving Mayor Warren Striker's name and number for reservations.

John Mansfield read the article to his nephew as the boy watched his caged pet. When finished he said, "You certainly take a good picture."

He handed the paper over to Chase. "Do you think other people will want a feeder?" asked the boy.

"I think so," said the uncle.

"If they do," asked Chase. "Will they be feeding other animals that are friends with Humphrey?"

His mother Julia was present and said, "Of course. Humphrey is well known to animals *everywhere.* Just remember," she said. "You have to find a home for him soon because he *needs* to be living outside."

The boy looked at the squirrel in the cage. It was standing up and scratching on the screen. Chase knew that it wanted to be set free. "I will, mom," he said. "First I need to find him a good home."

Monday morning at Striker Headquarters

Peter Constantine met Warren Striker as he was unlocking his office. "Did you read yesterday's paper?" he asked.

"Which copy?" replied the mayor. "When I read the article I bought every issue my neighborhood store had." He opened the door with each taking off their coats and hanging them in a closet. The mayor sat behind his desk with Peter taking a chair that faced him.

"We have victory, my friend!" exclaimed Peter as he held his copy over his head.

Warren looked down at his answering machine and saw that it was full. "My gosh," he said. "People must be calling in about it already."

He started to play back a recording. "Mayor Striker, my name is Marsha Jones from Huntington. I would like to place an order for a Mea..."

Warren skipped to another message. "My name is, Claude Raymond and I was wondering how much a package for The Mea..."

He skipped to another message. "Hi, this is Bill Schultise from Millstown. I was wondering if anyone could assist me in getting information about a Meadowdale Experience Package. It's for my..." Warren turned off the recording machine and leaned back in his chair.

"Well," said the mayor. "The word certainly got out there."

"Run with the ball," advised Peter.

Looking back he said, "You're right. That's why we did this. I'll have to contact the community center and possibly draw up a contract."

"Full speed ahead!" remarked Peter as he saluted Warren.

"I might as well go down there and congratulate everyone on the production they did and see what I can negotiate." Looking at Peter with his *I could use a friend about now* "look" he asked, "Care to join me?"

"I wouldn't miss it for the world," came his reply.

The phone began to ring. Pointing at it, he told Peter, "Don't answer."

———

Mayor Warren Striker and Peter were soon *talking turkey* with choice members of the MCC.

"This has the makings to jump start this entire town," stressed the mayor. "We can sell packages that will bring customers to our hotels, restaurants, shops and greatly help the MCC financially."

"It makes complete sense to me," remarked Andy.

"We had fun doing it last week," said Steve. "We can get a good system down and put out a lot of feeders."

"I agree," said John. "Everyone here has the spirit to make this happen."

"They'll really get into it," commented Julie.

"We already have a lot of requests," said Peter. "Is it possible to have a few feeders made in a week?"

"Absolutely no problem," said Steve. "All we need is the material to make it plus a maximum time of one week."

"We certainly have enough people to do it," giggled Renée

"Hey," said Warren. "Are we able to have two presentations a week right here? If the MCC would give the same performance they just did on every Friday and Saturday night, we just might be able to keep up with the demand."

"They would love it," said Andy.

"I can write more plays and sing other songs too," added Renée

"Well then," said Warren. "Shall we go to the homeroom and take a vote?"

"Good idea," said John.

The homeroom was full of electricity when they entered. They all saw Sunday's paper and arrived in jubilation. When Mayor Warren Striker and Peter Constantine appeared, their feeling of accomplishment skyrocketed. Warren and Peter walked to the front of the class and opened up with a hearty congratulations.

Mayor Striker held up the front page that everyone was familiar with and spoke."You guys did a fantastic job representing this town to our governor for a second time!"

Everyone cheered.

"Splendid job," added Peter. "Splendid!"

"Look," said the mayor. "What we're trying to say is that the entire town of Meadowdale is proud of all of you. What you did to represent yourselves at the Governor's Day Celebration and the great performance you gave last Saturday put us on the map." Warren Striker had more to say.

"The feeder that came from this building; the very one that every one of you touched is gaining popularity. In fact, there are people asking if you would be willing to build feeders for them just as you did for our governor. They will even *pay* for it and spend some time in this town meeting people like yourself and others who live here."

"This can turn into a business," he explained waving his hook. Looking at every set of eyes before him, he pointed out more probabilities. "The MCC and the entire town can get upgraded with the revenue this could bring in. While we do this endeavor we're still helping the community, having fun and making others happy too."

Warren noticed Andy looking intently with his arms folded. The man in the wheelchair nodded with full understanding about the importance of this presentation.

"Let's vote on this," said the elected official. "Anyone who doesn't want to build any more feeders and not do presentations for the town of Meadowdale, raise your hand."

Not one hand was raised.

With confidence, the mayor asked. "Raise your hand if you want to do what you did last Saturday, every Friday and Saturday here on out."

Every hand in the room was raised including one hook.

"Let's make Meadowdale Feeders!" cried out Warren Striker. The entire room cheered and applauded with the realization that *Meadowdale needed them.* Using his cell phone, Warren Striker ordered pizza and pop as a 'thank you' to the entire MCC. He waited for the food to arrive and had one slice of pizza. Peter wanted to spend the rest of the day at the MCC with Steve Smith offering him a ride home.

This change worked out well because Warren had plans to join Christine Bratton for lunch. An engagement he wouldn't forget a second time. Soon he was at the designated cafe with a beautiful woman wearing a Meadowdale Patriots awards jacket from years past. The special was a bacon, lettuce and tomato sandwich with potato salad and ice tea, with each the nod.

"I saw the presentation at the community center," she said. "It was incredible! Everyone loved it!"

"I liked it too," remarked Warren.

"Everyone in town is also talking about Sunday's paper," she added. "They all loved it."

"Well, good," said Warren. "It seems that Sunday's article did what it was meant to."

"What do you mean?" asked Christine as she took a bite of her sandwich.

"This morning I was swamped with orders," he explained. "I didn't realize that we would have that many customers so soon. I probably need to hire someone to answer the calls and coordinate things with Roger, Terry and the community center." Warren took a drink of ice tea and looked away in thought.

"When do I start?" she asked.

Putting his glass down he looked at her, "Are you serious?"

"Sure I am," she replied. "Are you forgetting that I also live in Meadowdale and believe in this town? Besides, there were times when Roger and Terry were short on staff and had me taking reservations. I also liked what I saw at the MCC and already met Renée and Julia." Taking a sip of her drink she continued. "I read the article this Sunday and understand that it's all about receiving whatever the customer wants to use for their feeder, then allow the community center the time to construct it."

Warren listened intently, nodding his head in agreement.

"This will work out just fine," she assured.

Warren retorted. "What I need to do now is to bring all of the players together so that we can agree on a schedule."

The couple finished their meal with Christine asking, "So when do I start?"

Warren looked at her and answered, "How about...now?"

The man with the hook received a kiss on his cheek. "Proud to serve," she said.

The next night the town of Meadowdale conducted a meeting in the banquet room at Hart's Diner. Those who ran the MCC, Roger Green and his wife, Terry and Candice Hart along with Peter, Warren and Christine were all present. "I'm glad that you could all attend," said Mayor Striker.

Everyone understood about the process needed to provide a customer The Meadowdale Experience. It was agreed that the MCC would only accept twenty orders a month knowing that they had the work force and resources to easily accomplish the task. From there, an order would be added once one was finished.

The client would be notified once their feeder was created. At that moment, they would pick what Friday or Saturday they wanted the MCC to give their presentation. As far as anyone was concerned, it didn't matter how many feeders were presented on a given night. *The more, the merrier* was their motto.

The Meadowdale Experience Package was anything from staying one night, to an entire week- unless the party wanted to stay even longer. It was whatever the visitor from out of town wanted, just as long as they stayed at least one night to *experience* Meadowdale.

An obvious question was raised by John Mansfield. "How much do we charge for a package?"

Warren looked away preoccupied in thought. "You don't have to worry about a thing," he said. "I'll take care of it."

Everyone *knew* that side of Warren Striker. They had no doubts that he would get the town of Meadowdale *a good deal.*

CHAPTER XXII

The addition of Christine Bratton to the mayor's staff was huge. She contacted all who inquired about the Meadowdale Package and explained how the rotating waiting list worked. Last, she gave the honor of having the customer talk to, or in some circumstances actually meet the popular mayor with the shiny hook.

This was where Warren Robert Striker read their palm by nonchalantly asking a few generic questions. Words like gift, support and donation were cleverly used in his dialogue. Compliments that massaged egos seasoned the pot.

After the ice was broken and introductions were made, Warren Striker began *to sell cars.*

"No, no, no. Call me *Warren.*"

"A doctor whose retiring? Hey, are you available for meeting me for lunch?"

"So your parents want to celebrate their fiftieth anniversary doing the Meadowdale Experience?"

"You own a steel mill you say?"

"Wow! I have always wondered how anyone could do such a sophisticated job like that."

"You played semi-pro baseball for two years? I bet every major league team in the nation wanted you."

Christine loved listening to Warren talk to the customers. It did her good seeing that some things never change.

Meanwhile, at the MCC in Meadowdale, USA

The word was out that the MCC was in the business of making Meadowdale Feeders. As always, its open door policy encouraged any who wanted to take part.

Andy and the gang noticed the growing members of the community center and in a round-about way created *two shifts.* They simply kept the doors open until eight and staggered their arrival time.

The procedure became relatively simple.

It started off with Steve and John contacting Christine to send materials for an order when a previous one was complete.

Once the artifacts arrived, they were spread out on a table for members to survey. From there, each would attempt to draw a configuration of modern art they felt would best represent the customer. Without fail, everyone seemed to stumble and scratch their head trying to mentally envision a classic feeder.

Chase, on the other hand, would glance at the scattered keepsakes and within moments sketch another *Picasso.*

Once a design was accepted, the pieces chosen were immediately cleaned by volunteers. If anything needed to be chrome plated, Steve would ship it out and have it returned within three days.

Steve and John were good welders and would assemble the current feeder according to design. Once assembled, the MCC would beautify it with their painting, polishing and love. Because of the massive work force, the community center divided itself into groups and could easily put out at least five personal feeders a week.

There was more.

The very crew that created a certain feeder took a group picture that was signed and framed. This wall hanging was included as part of the gift.

Fridays and Saturdays were show time. A short play utilizing every member from the MCC would take place followed by Renée singing two ballets. As always, the Meadowdale High School Band was present in full force. Then it was 'game show time' with everyone in suspense.

That Friday, things were hopping in Meadowdale. Three classic car clubs arrived in town for the weekend. Their rods would be displayed in town for three days with their members waiting to watch the MCC perform. Christine made a suggestion to Warren.

"Roger and the gang want to thank you for giving them lots of business. They want to take us out for Chinese food as a "Thank you," and then go to the car show. After that they wanted to go to the MCC and watch their presentation."

"Now *that* sounds like a fun time!" responded Warren. "Can we invite Peter?"

"He was already invited," said Christine.

Friday found Warren Striker with his girlfriend, Christine sitting in the MCC auditorium with their friends. They were just early enough to get front row seats as the place started to fill up.

"Dinner was great," commented Warren.

The show started with Renée's play, *Neighborly Prayers.* It was slightly modified with a touch of humor added. Once finished the entire room stood up and cheered the many seniors and disadvantaged that performed. Next she sang two Mama and Papa ballets with an equal ovation calling for one more: *California Dreaming.*

It was now game time with the lights out, music playing and spotlights buzzing the crowd. All at once a light was fixed on none-other than Warren Striker himself. Steve Smith's familiar voice called out: "Mayor Warren Striker, come ooonn down!"

It was a set-up with the entire house going nuts. Out of nowhere came John and Julia Mansfield as they escorted the latest contestant to the stage. The local politician who was always aware of his surroundings was caught off guard.

With megaphone in hand, Steve addressed him. "Welcome, Mayor Striker."

"Thank you," said Warren. "You're not getting me arrest are you?" The audience loved his humor and laughed.

"No, at least I don't think so," volleyed back the master of ceremony.

With top hat standing tall and speaker positioned towards the audience, Steve began to recite the 'Meadowdale Feeder Vows.'

"Warren Robert Striker, do you solemnly swear to love, honor and feed your Meadowdale Feeder for as long as you live?"

It just dawned on Warren that *he* was going to receive a feeder that was making his town famous. "Oh, you better believe it," he assured.

The man in tails continued. "What about for richer or poor?"

"I'll still be true," he replied.

"And in sickness or in health?"

"I'll nurse it back to health when needed," promised the man with one hook.

Steve looked at the crowd and asked. "Well...what do you think?"

Many cheers came back with those saying:

"Give it to him!"

"Let him have it!"

"Give that Meadowdale Feeder a home!"

Steve obeyed the crowd's request and boldly announced: "By the power invested in me I now proclaim you as the proud father of a seventy-pound ten-ounce Meadowdale Feeder!"

Christine came out from the far side of the stage wearing her Meadowdale Patriots jacket. With sledgehammer in hand, she nailed the bullseye with full force.

Bwwaaaamm!

The music started to play as the curtain opened. The whole room screamed and yelled with Warren Robert Striker seeing what he was always denied.

It wasn't the glistening chrome plated Meadowdale Feeder made out of the 1959 Edsel he once drove. The one that eventually became a classic for the true car collector.

The entire MCC was present in the background wearing shirts that identified each member. It wasn't them, however, nor his friends who posed as a human pyramid.

It was a certain someone standing just behind his gift that drove him to success. An individual who was standing right next to his mother. A person that displayed what he would look like twenty years from now.

It was his father. The one who cursed him for not playing on the high school football team. The mentor who shunned him for not having an illustrious military career and disgracing the family name during a brief stint with a car dealership. The man who always told him that he'd *never amount to anything.*

His outlook towards his son had changed. He was holding last Sunday's newspaper that had his son's picture with the governor. Waving the newsprint he pointed towards him saying the words he longed to hear. "That's my son! My son is Mayor Warren Robert Striker! I'm so proud of you—the entire country knows who you are!"

Warren's mother added a comment. "You were always a winner!"

Emotion took control over the son with one hand. Without any thought, acceptance and forgiveness came through his heart.

"Dad," you look great!" Warren's dad ran up to him giving that long-overdue hug his son needed years ago.

The proud father could not stop giving recognition to his boy. "Hey, everybody, this is my son!"

It was customary for those in the audience to join those on stage. This was to introduce oneself to the guest of honor, meet the MCC and get a closer look at the latest Meadowdale Feeder. It was also a heyday for the local news and traveling reporters.

What was waiting was breathtaking.

An enclosed frame held the tall grill from the 1959 Ford that lettered *Edsel* from top to bottom. On either side of the grill were the original headlights encased in their authentic chrome casings. In front was the car's polished hubcaps that rested inches off the ground, serving as two feeding bowls with lids. The two settings had their covers secured six inches above. This allowed access to the food and water while serving as a protective shield. Again, the name 'Edsel' was printed on each hub, matching the grill.

The centerpiece was the unmistakable blue steering column with gear selector still intact. Its classic, matching steering wheel was resting on top in its usual position with the name 'Edsel' once again, proudly displayed. The rear had its original red tail lights positioned properly, gleaming as if they just left the factory.

Steve Smith joined in by saying, "And don't forget about this." He moved the gear selector on the steering column causing the front and back lights to turn on.

Bill Riggens, the president of the 'Slick 50s Car Club' was almost drooling over the vintage Edsel parts. He got out his checkbook and wrote out a large amount as an offer to buy the feeder. He handed the check to Warren, a man who had moments of financial struggle. Looking at the figure, he noticed the series of zeros. This made his eyes bulge. It was enough to pay off his house and put a little extra into his retirement.

At that moment, Warren's dad called out. "Peter, thanks for getting us all together."

Peter shared the bottom of the human pyramid and was catching his breath. He shook hands with Mr. Striker and hugged both parents saying, "Good show." Looking at Warren he said, "You have wonderful parents."

Seeing his friend, Peter made him realize all the things he did for his life, thus making his Meadowdale Feeder *priceless.*

With dignity, the mayor handed back the check saying, "I'm sorry, but I will *never* sell it." He did, however, promise to loan it out whenever the Slick 50s wanted to display it. "It will help everyone," said Warren. "Including Meadowdale."

CHAPTER XXIII

W arren Striker had a good Saturday. He attended the car show again, but this time with with his mother and father. They marveled at his *Edsel themed* Meadowdale Feeder that was on display with Sparkles. Many had the mayor pose with his parents while taking pictures of it. The family also went out to dinner and watched the MCC present two more feeders. He was at peace with the updated relationship with his father.

Still, a new problem arose.

Feeling that his hook had been replaced with the technology of a Meadowdale Feeder, he would try once again, to feed Maxwell *manually*.

Within the confinements of his own backyard, he assumed the usual position on the corner of his deck. With arm fully extended, he leaned towards the furry resident. His shiny hook pierced the seasoned steak that awaited for the lone cat.

"Here, Maxwell. Heeere, kitty, kitty, kitty. C'mon, Maxwell; eat your dinner."

Kissing sounds accompanied his invitation.

"C'mon, kitty..."

The cat appeared more intellectual and remained *calm as a cucumber*.

More sappy kissing sounds were made as he leaned further towards the cat. "Here, Maxwell. Come get your steak..."

Unexpectedly, Peter's voice came from the back gate interrupting Warren's negotiation with the cat. "Do you mind if I come in?"

Warren recognized Peter's voice and turned towards him. "You never have to ask to come over," stated Warren. "In fact, I was going to call you tonight."

The mayor of Meadowdale began to thank Peter for his friendship. "It's not just that you got my father to take another look at me," he said. "It's all the little things you have done for me since we met."

Peter started to move his upper body in an unorthodox manner while remaining quiet. Warren thought that Peter's good nature was attempting to state his gratification in return and continued speaking.

"It was quite clear that I was trying to remove any creditability from you when we first met at the veteran's hall," he pointed out. "Then, when I got into hot water, you didn't pounce on me. Instead, you did everything you could to help me save face."

Peter was still making his erratic motions, obviously wanting to say something.

Warren was almost finished. "What I'm trying to say is that if I had to go through life having made only one friend, it would be *you*, Peter."

Peter was now waving his hands like a man stranded on an island spotting a plane. "What is it, Peter?"

He was at a loss for words and frantically pointed towards the mayor's hook. Warren turned and saw it was bare. Looking a few feet away was Maxwell savoring the last bite.

The MCC was gaining in popularity. It was common for magazine and newspaper articles to feature it with the name, Chase Mansfield constantly mentioned. The young man who created Sparkles was acquiring a celebrity status due to a few interviews and poses that went nationwide.

Still, he was only Chase Mansfield from Meadowdale. The very reason why he was loved so much.

The Meadowdale Community Center was the right image for America. Its small population consisted of all walks of life, with a special emphasis for seniors and the disadvantaged. It also took measures to preserve the environment by making it's famous feeders out of 'would-be scraps.'

Most importantly, it seemed to be *The Statue Of Liberty Of Meadowdale*. Widows, widowers, retirees and those handicapped wanted to live there like a kid dreaming about Disney Land. Nobody was excluded. Meadowdale and its MCC were for those who believed.

Chase Mansfield was intently cleaning parts for a Meadowdale Feeder on order. Andy entered the room with a bewildered looking old man who came from a far away place. He had a gray beard and wore tattered clothing. Andy called out to Chase. "Chase, can you come here for a moment?"

The youth put down his cleaning utensils and approached Andy and the stranger. "I'd like you to meet someone who traveled far to join us," said Andy. "Chase, this is Emmett Brooks and he's heard a lot about us."

Chase extended his hand while giving sincere eye contact. He introduced himself, "Hi, Emmett, my name is Chase Mansfield."

The old man who appeared to be in his late seventies reached into his back pocket. With trembling hands, he removed a folded up magazine article that he cut out and saved. He unfolded a picture of Chase and held it next to the boy's face to assure identity.

"It's you," he exclaimed. "You really are Chase Mansfield!"

Chase was amused. As far as he was concerned he wasn't anyone special. He did, however, like Emmett and wanted to know him. "Can I ask you a favor?" asked the sweet old man.

"Sure," answered Chase.

"I've got no one," he said. "When I heard about you, the community center and this town, I came straight here. Can I join in with you and your friends and help make those famous feeders?"

"That would be fun, Emmett," said Chase. "You'll like it here."

The man started to clap his hands while high-stepping. "Yippee!" he cheered. "I made it! I am now a part of the Meadowdale Community center!"

Andy extended his hand and shook Emmett's. "Welcome aboard," he said. "Everyone is going to love you."

On occasion, an "Emmett Brooks" would appear at the MCC with a look hope in their eyes. Soon, such a person would have a home and wear a bright colored MCC shirt with their name printed on it.

CHAPTER XXIV

S mall towns aren't without their sense of humor. Against contrary belief, they have greatly evolved since *Prince Albert in a can.*

Mayor Warren Striker arrived earlier than usual at the office. It was Monday, and he had several meetings to prepare for. He was also aware of the many requests that Christine had to handle and wanted to lighten her load.

He began to replay a few 'Meadowdale Feeder requests' and wrote down the vital information given. When he reviewed the fourth order he dropped his pen saying, "No, this can't be." Despite a growing number of rumors circulating around town, it was still too far-fetched. *"Kids,"* he muttered to himself.

Paul Blades arrived at his desk with visitors present requesting to see his uncle. His voice projected through the intercom. "Uncle, Warren," he said in a quivery voice. "There are some people here to see you."

The mayor reached over the intercom and pressed the button that would allow him to transmit. "Send them in," he responded as he scanned documents that were left on his desk.

Finally, he looked up and froze in disbelief. The message he regarded as a prank was no joke at all. There standing before him was *Balsam Alberto and the V-O Fives.* A world-renowned multiethnic band out of Seattle. They were in their famous *'V' for victory* stance waiting patiently for the mayor to share some of his time. Warren was overwhelmed and commented, "So, you guys really are in town."

The *Beatles* had arrived in Meadowdale.

Alberto stood closest. In 'V-O Five fashion,' he matched his band members by wearing a 'do-wop' hairstyle from the 50s. Their clothing had its bright colors that were a little *Sgt. Pepperish*. The entire band was present: Victor, Rico, Stanley, Glenn and 'Balsam Alberto' himself. "We are the V-O Fives and want to experience Meadowdale," said Alberto with his mild Hispanic accent.

Warren activated the intercom and spoke into it. "Paul, cancel all of my appointments for the rest of the day."

"Right away," came the response.

At that moment, Christine entered the office. It only took a millisecond for her to recognize the music icons. She stood still with her mouth wide open. With all of his charm, Alberto introduced himself. "My name is Alberto and I'd like you to meet the V-O Fives."

Christine fainted.

This was a common occurrence that the famous band was not proud of. They did, however, make up for it when possible. The secretary was carried to a sofa in the room and had a damp cloth placed over her forehead. She came around in good spirits with Warren and the visitors relieved. "I hope you can spend the day with us," said a warm Alberto.

Warren saw his high school crush being offered the dream every teenager wished for. "You bet she can," came his reply. Looking at their guests, he asked. "Is there any place in particular you guys would like to start?"

"We're glad you asked us that," said the naturalized citizen from south of the border. His drummer, Stanley Adoyo, was holding a folded newspaper print that reached their neck of the woods. The native from Kenya handed it to the band leader. Alberto displayed the article to the mayor. It was about the town of

Meadowdale *coming alive* with Chase Mansfield being featured. A picture of Chase posing with Sparkles was included. "We love feeding animals and want to meet Chase Mansfield," said Alberto.

Each member gave their two-cents worth.

"Chase is that guy we want to be like," said bass player, Rico Sanchez from South America.

"Chase Mansfield has started a movement about caring for others, and it includes the less fortunate and animals," remarked Glenn Fletcher, their keyboard player from Canada.

Stanley spoke up. "We took a brief stop on our tour with the hopes that we could meet him."

"Chase is *my man,*" said their guitarist, Victor Black from Nebraska.

Nothing more needed to be said. It was off to the MCC!

While leaving the mayor's office, Alberto made a suggestion. "How about riding with us? Our limousine has plenty of room." In 'rock-star' fashion, the group of seven drove to the MCC.

Once there, the view from their parking space reminded Alberto of his childhood. The MCC was an outdated structure that was held together by the labor of love. Festive artwork displayed on faded white paint served as a band-aid for the deteriorating community center. It was just like the small village he grew up in. Nobody was aware that it was declared poverty because they were happy. In their eyes, they had *everything*. Getting out of the limo, he walked up to a wall that displayed an array of hand prints. Like any child, he started to match his hand over the imprints until he found one that matched his perfectly.

He studied the many paintings of horses, cattle, barns and people. "*Just like home,*" he thought to himself. Once inside the omnipresence of lower income continued. Uneven murals and framed pictures of yesterday's classes further hid the building's decomposing process. Finally, they entered the homeroom where a spirited community emerged. What Alberto and his band members discovered was a collection of seniors and those of special needs. Regardless of age, ethnic background, or handicap, all were interacting in harmony. 'Balsam Alberto' and his friends felt at home.

The late arrivals were fortunate and found just enough available seats grouped together. Few recognized the legendary band, but those who did tensed up in disbelief. Steve gave a nudge to get Allen's attention while Julia, John and Andy gave a 'double take.' There were others that did their best not make their guests feel uncomfortable. Peter knew who everyone was and grinned at Warren in approval.

'Social time' was on the verge of being introduce with the V-O Fives watching with curiosity.

Ella Ray and Lois Sexton teamed up and approached the gathering from the upper corner of the room. Wearing dark sunglasses with hands clasped behind their backs, they slowly swaggered into the room. Ella would suddenly stop and stare at someone just a few feet away while maintaining a poker face. Lois would follow suit giving someone else a stern look. This process continued for about two minutes with the entire room in suspense. Ella made a slight motion then all at once they threw candy in the air yelling, "It's social time!"

The two-woman show received an applause for their well-rehearsed act. At that time, Andy wheeled up to the band, introduced himself and explained what social time was. He insisted that they be first in line at the dessert table and meet everyone.

"I like it here!" commented Rico.

In time, all were served with the regulars taking time to visit the newcomers with the 50's style.

Finally, Chase Mansfield made his way through the crowd and introduced himself to Alberto. "I know who you are," said the special needs student. "I watch you on TV and listen to you on the radio."

Alberto had a tear run down his cheek. He realized that Chase wasn't 'star-struck' despite his fame. The fifteen-year-old was too pure for that. He simply knew enough about Alberto and his band to genuinely like him. "Well, hey," replied Alberto. "I know who you are, too."

Alberto engaged in a conversation with Chase by asking sincere questions. The international celebrity wanted to further understand the boy he held so much respect for. While they conversed, his band members asked Warren Striker what they needed to do to get Alberto a Meadowdale Feeder. "It's for the band's fifth anniversary," explained Victor. "We were hoping to surprise him with one before we leave town."

"Follow me," said Warren. Soon they were in the art room with Andy, Renée and the others that coordinated the MCC activities.

Glenn spoke up and took a roll of paper money out of his pocket. "We know that the feeders bring in revenue to help this town." Handing the undisclosed amount of cash to the mayor he said, "Let me know if more is needed."

The former car dealer knew how to calculate the weight of paper money and commented. "This will do just fine." Looking at Steve, he asked. "Can they be next in line since they are leaving town soon?"

"We'll jump on it first thing once we get the materials," said Steve.

Stanley said, "We have one of our moving vans in town that has the things we already selected for Alberto's feeder."

"Bring it to the loading dock in the back of this building, and we'll get started," said John.

"We appreciate this so-much," said Stanley.

Looking at Warren, Steve said, "It will be ready for this Friday's first presentation."

The mayor looked at the band and asked, "How much time do you guys have?"

"We plan on getting a hotel room and staying here until Sunday," replied Rico.

Christine took over. "Your hotel room is taken care of," she said. "Just give me a few minutes." The competent secretary walked a few feet away and dialed her cell phone.

"Meadowdale Hotel, this is Roger."

"You're kidding me!"

"Yes, we heard the talk going around town but...*The V-O Fives?*"

"They'll have our best room. I'll set it up right now."

"Okay, I'll let them know."

"You, too, Chris, and Thanks!"

It was time for the entertainers to check into the Meadowdale Hotel and 'take in Meadowdale.'

Within two hours, Steve and John had the musical artifacts spread on a table. It was now time to bring in the MCC members and submit ideas.

Everyone walked around the bench table and viewed the brass horns, bongos, microphones, worn string instruments and pieces from various drum sets. Attempts were partially made that went nowhere. After twenty minutes of scratched out ideas, it was time to bring in the cavalry. "Will someone get Chase?" called out Andy.

"I know where he is," replied Allen. He left and returned with the master designer.

Chase looked at the instruments on the table and asked a question. "Where are they from?"

"Seattle," answered his mother.

"Can you show me any pictures of Seattle?" he asked.

His mother took out her cell phone and googled the name of the city. She retrieved a series of pictures that illustrated the Emerald City and showed them to her son. The first one was the Space Needle. "What's that?" he asked.

"It's called the Space Needle" and is a place where you can eat great meals and view the city," she explained.

Taking a closer look at the picture he had another question. "Can the top part of it fly?"

"Well, the inside of it does turn," pointed out his uncle, John.

"Wow," said Chase. "That's neat."

More pictures were shown that included the famous football team with the youth marveling at their striking blue and green colors. Next, he noticed the number *12* being displayed on shirts, flags, houses and practically *everything*. It caught his attention making him ask his uncle what it meant.

John Mansfield began to explain. "That number represents the millions of fans who follow the Seahawks. Since they are only allowed to have eleven players on the field during a game, the number *twelve* means that the fans are also included."

"Like us?" he questioned. "We allow everyone to be with us too."

"Right," agreed John, "and they're also champions, just like us."

Chase loved his answer.

Andy handed him a pad and pencil saying, "See what you can come up with."

Chase walked around the table when suddenly an idea came to mind. He isolated himself in a nearby chair and began to create. Those present remained quiet.

He spent almost ten minutes with a result well worth the wait. He returned and placed his concept on the table for all to see. "What do you think?" he asked.

It was obvious that the Space Needle and the champion Seahawks left an impression. He centered his work around a tall polished stem that had a pedal on the bottom with two matching cymbals on top. A design that remotely resembled the famous landmark. Three brass trombones met in the middle and branched downward in opposite directions. Three more met in the middle and followed suit to the 'Hi-hat' cymbals. The wind instruments were now the massive girders that supported the rotating restaurant. A microphone stuck out just below the cymbals with a pair of stainless steel bongo drums inches off the bottom.

Chase added a final touch:

The number *12* was written front and center on the top cymbal.

Andy knew what he was looking at. His eyes grew twice its size realizing that Chase Mansfield possessed a rare gift. *He was a natural artistic genius.*

"Nothing here needs foundry work," said Steve. "Let's get everybody in here to clean it. I'll have it welded together sometime tomorrow."

CHAPTER XXV

The town of Meadowdale was laced with activity.

At one end, the MCC was busy polishing brass and shining stainless steel. The *Seattle rendition* of the latest Meadowdale Feeder was getting its final touch with Seahawk colors being applied by loving hands. The rest of the town was a different story. Groupies were searching high and low for Balsam Alberto And The V-O Fives.

It was time for the band to split up and take cover. They would now adapt to their 'jeans and t-shirt mode' with each walking a different direction. Somewhere in a secluded teriyaki restaurant, Alberto Ribas (aka Balsam Alberto) was in his street clothes having lunch with one Peter Constantine. He wore a farm hat and had his back turned to the windows. The only face visible was Peter's, giving the illusion that the superstar was elsewhere. Balsam Alberto was safely harbored.

"It's amazing what you have to do to get some privacy," commented Peter.

"We love our fans and don't mind it at all," said Alberto.

Peter's accent reminded the musician of himself. "It was always tough for guys like us to claim being an American with our accents."

"Tell me about it," remarked Peter. "When I meet someone, they ask me how long I'll be staying in the country. They don't even know that I fought a war for them." He looked away sipping his tea.

"I go through the same thing," he said. "There were times when someone asked to see my green card when I lived in the country longer than they have." Alberto took a bite of his food as he laughed to himself.

Peter nodded with a full understanding.

There were other things that the two had in common. Alberto's dance steps on stage and slight list when he walked always passed as being 'normal.' In actuality, his right leg was slightly shorter than his left. It was much like

Peter's eye patch, but drew less attention.

The Bavarian man was also very sensitive: just like Alberto Ribas. They both *cared* about others.

"What do you like to do?" asked Alberto.

Peter swallowed his food and took another drink. "Believe it or not," he said. "I use to play in a band back home."

"Really? What kind of band?"

"Polka music," answered Peter.

"Wow, that's great, Peter! What instruments did you play?"

"The Clarinet, flute, trumpet and sometimes a kettle drum," answered Peter.

Alberto slapped his hand on the table. "I love those instruments!" he claimed. "That's what I started off playing."

The meal was finished with Peter grabbing the check. Alberto wanted to buy. After all, he made more in one concert than Peter took home in five years. Besides, he cherished the man.

"Next time you can get it," was the host's response.

The check was paid with a respectable tip waiting for the server. They decided to visit longer and had their tea cups topped-off. "What did you do back home growing up?" asked Peter.

"My family had a *cantina* where I helped out after school." Alberto looked around and said, "It was a place like this." The server walked by with the superstar incognito asking a question. "Do you mind if I take a look inside your kitchen? Your restaurant is like the one we have back home."

The server was also the owner and didn't have a problem with the request. Alberto expressed his gratitude and walked towards the kitchen with Peter following. Peering through the doorway the familiar sight of industrial-sized pots and pans rested above an open flame. Looking at the counter something caught Alberto's eye. It was a Veg-O-Matic with vegetables waiting to be diced. Pointing at the instrument he called out to Peter. "Hey, look what they got. My mother won one of those things on a game show!"

That evening Chase Mansfield was at home with his mother and uncle. They broke out all of their V-O Five music and played it loud while dancing in the living room. Finally, they were worn out, having had their exercise for the day. "What do we do for dinner?" asked John.

"Can we go out for pizza?" asked Chase.

"That sounds good," said Julia.

"Let's get cleaned up and we'll meet in the car," said John.

"Can we ask Alberto and his friends if they want to join us?" asked Chase.

Julia looked at her brother and knew the odds of that. "How about I call Mayor Striker and leave him a message? I will let him know that we're going to Benard's for pizza, and he can let everyone know. I'm sure they'll come if they are available."

"Okay, mom," answered Chase.

Julia made the call in front of her son. Regardless of what happened, at least he knew that his mother tried.

The window of opportunity proved to be open. Warren was at the hotel where the band reunited. Roger, Terry and the rest of the gang happened to be in the lobby with them. The mayor listened to his message and immediately called out. "Hey everybody, Chase Mansfield wants to meet all of us at Benard's for pizza!"

"Chase called for us?" commented Alberto in a surprised tone. "The most popular guy in town wants to have pizza with *us?*" "Let's do it, and bring my man, Peter!"

The V-O Fives unanimously favored the motion.

"Chase! Chase! Chase!" they cheered.

The Mansfields arrived at Benard's to see a full parking lot, two news teams and screaming teens. "Why are there so many people here?" asked Chase.

"It's probably because your friends are here," said his uncle.

How right he was.

They were forced to park across the street and down one block. Arriving in the parking lot, they could see a shiny hook at the front door waving for them to enter. The crowd respected the mayor and, recognizing Chase, divided to allow entry. "Word certainly gets around here fast," said Mayor Striker in a joking way. Warren greeted John and Julia at the door with handshakes and hugs. Placing a hand and a hook on either side of Chase's shoulders Warren said, "This was a great idea, Chase."

Once inside a table of ten awaited for them that included the five legendary rock stars. "Is Peter coming?" asked Alberto.

"He's on his way," said Warren.

Looking through the window, Alberto saw his friend crossing the street and walking towards the mob. Without any thought, he gave the crowd what they wanted: an appearance. Walking to the front door, screams were heard, microphones hovered above him, and pictures were being snapped. "There's my man, Pete!" he exclaimed.

Peter heard what Alberto called him: *Pete*. That was a shortened rendition of his first name; the way a friend would address another. What made more of an impact was that his friend was one of the most famous people on the planet. *Balsam Alberto* himself. This icon called him, "Pete" in front of live cameras. The crowd respected Alberto's request about letting his friend through, with autograph seekers getting their immortal signature.

In front of all, Alberto Ribas identified his friend, 'Pete Constantine,' with the whole world watching. "Get in here, Pete!" He shook Peter's hand, then playfully wrestled with him. Peter was never 'one of the guys' before, but took to it quickly. When it dawned on him that Alberto was playing with him the way 'buds' do, he got the star in a loose headlock and patted his head twice.

The press and fans loved it. So did someone else very special to Peter. Warren saw everything through the dining room window and gave a thumbs-up to his classy friend.

The Pizza with friends was fantastic. Fans were allowed to enter the room one-at-a time to meet the V-O Fives along with a popular Chase Mansfield. Briefly, they took pictures with the idols and got autographs.

"It's just like the Seahawk's *twelfth man,*" pointed out Chase. "Everyone is a part of this."

His comment was profound and registered deeply with the Seattle band. "Your exactly right, Brother Chase," said *Balsam* Alberto.

CHAPTER XXVI

Word continued to spread on how much fun the town of Meadowdale was. More people began to make the pilgrimage since the well-publicized appearance of the V-O Fives. There was more to this spirited town than the free production put on by the MCC. It was also known for its surprises.

Friday night arrived with a packed house.

It only took one visit to learn that arriving early gave best odds of getting a seat. Late arrivals were victims of standing room only. Everyone who went to the MCC that night was able to watch the production without an inch to spare.

Warren Striker utilized his clout and wisely reserved enough front row seats to accommodate his friends and family. It was important to have Alberto situated just right. Unbeknownst to him a Meadowdale Feeder awaited. Soon Renée and Andy came on stage, formally introducing themselves. They gave a briefing on what the community center was trying to accomplish with the play getting underway.

Practice makes perfect. The play, along with Renée's ballets, resulted with a standing ovation that lasted minutes. Then the lights went out with The Meadowdale High School Band playing the presentation's theme song.

Stage lights circled the entire audience with the surprised guest being pin-pointed. It was the famous 'Balsam Alberto' himself.

His newly acquainted friend, Steve Smith was ready for him. In true form, the resident 'MC' wearing the traditional top hat called out through the vintage megaphone. "Balsam Alberto, come ooonn down!"

Fans went crazy as their hero was escorted by John and Julia Mansfield to the stage. The first recipient of the night was stunned. He knew of the Meadowdale Feeder presentation, but never witnessed one before. He loved it!

Steve's quick wit kept the famous contestant on his toes, with the audience howling. Comments like:

"So tell me, Alberto, what do you do for a living?"

"Do you know of any good hair products?" had people rolling in the aisles.

Steve pulled out his scroll and began to recite The Meadowdale Feeder Vows.

"Do you solemnly swear to love, honor and feed your Meadowdale Feeder for as long as you live?"

Alberto was cracking up and said, "I do."

The man in tails continued. "What about in sickness and in health?"

"Sure," replied Alberto.

"And what about for richer or poorer?"

"I promise," he vowed.

Steve stood straight up and continued to read his script:

"By the power vested in me by the town of Meadowdale, I now pronounce you the proud father of a fifty-eight pound, four-ounce, Meadowdale Feeder!"

Out of nowhere appeared Peter. He was on the far left of the stage holding a sledgehammer. Swiftly, he nailed the bullseye dead center.

Bwwaaaaamm!

The curtain opened up with the theme song playing: *Da da da daa Da da da daa...*

The beautiful Space Needle-like feeder had been exposed with its stainless steel bongos ready to feed the animal kingdom. It was a gem.

The contestant immediately saw his band in their famous "V formation" with Peter filling in for him. Behind was the MCC members who proudly assembled Alberto's feeder.

The compassionate star began to cry. "Thanks, guys," he called out. "Thank you, everybody."

At that moment, Alberto remembered that he had a surprise feeder waiting for someone very special. "Okay," he said. "We have more festivities coming." He took the feeder and carried it off stage to a safe place. Peter and the V-O Fives took their seats in the audience.

The curtains closed with the lights going out.

It was *round two* with music playing and spotlights swirling.

Da da da daa Da da da daa...

All at once, a light glued itself to a bald head wearing an eye patch. Peter Constantine was now living the dream of every man, woman and child from his village.

"Peter Constantine, *come ooonn down!*"

Da da da daa Da da da daa...

Slapping his knee, the foreign-born contestant stood up raising both arms in victory. He *ran* to the stage. Steve was amused watching the senior jump up and down while clapping like a cheerleader.

"Welcome, Peter," greeted the MC. "Is it just me, or are you glad to be here?"

The audience cheered.

Peter clasped his hands together. "I have waited my whole life for this moment!" He was serious.

"Well good," replied Steve. He pulled out the scroll and began to recite the sacred oath. "Do you, Peter Constantine, solemnly swear to love honor and feed your Meadowdale Feeder for as long as you live?"

Looking up towards the heavens, he covered his mouth in ecstasy. Taking a deep breath, he opened up his hands saying, "Yes, yes, yes...I do!"

"How about for richer or poorer?" asked Steve.

Peter pointed his index finger to the sky. With conviction, he said, "I will never abandon my Meadowdale Feeder. *Never!*"

"And in sickness and in health?"

"I will clean it and feed it once a day!" he vowed.

Steve turned to the audience and opened his arms. "Well, do you think he will provide a good home for his Meadowdale feeder?"

The crowd went crazy!

"Let him take it home!"

"He'll be the best dad ever!"

"Go Peter! Go!"

The room started to chant his name.

"Peter! Peter! Peter! Peter! Peter!"

Steve completed the vows. "By the authority vested in me by the township of Meadowdale, I now pronounce you the proud father of a one-hundred and one pound three-ounce Meadowdale Feeder!"

Alberto entered from the far corner of the stage. Holding the sledgehammer, he took two practice swings and then nailed the center dot.

Bwaaaammmm!

The band started to play as the curtain opened.

What seemed like an eternity was only seconds as Peter twitched and fidgeted in suspense.

And then it happened:

Another *personal* Meadowdale Feeder was introduced to the world with the crowd sighing in awe.

"Ooooohh..."

Peter froze, realizing that the gold-plated, brass and chrome creation before him was *his*. One could say that it resembled a mini 'Leaning Tower Of Pisa' that stood erect, or a fountain that would serve as a centerpiece for any castle.

Six gold plated trumpets supported a brass kettle drum that was large enough to be a bird bath. They were welded on the sides of the drum, just low enough for the flared horns to touch the ground.

The top of the kettle had six chrome plated clarinets welded around the inside of the rim, supporting a matching kettle drum of smaller size. Six chrome plated flutes stood tall outlining the rim of the second kettle like sharp objects protecting the top of a wrought iron gate. Ingeniously, each layer of instruments were in line with the others.

The wind instruments and brass kettles definitely displayed 'a touch of Europe.' Peter was in a world of his own as he slowly walked up to his gift. Looking beyond he saw Warren, Alberto and his other friends shoulder-to-shoulder with the MCC members standing behind them in the same formation.

The show was over with those in the audience free to enter the stage. "I going to get my feeder and place it next to Peter's," said Alberto. Looking at Peter, he said, "I appreciate this so much, brother."

Peter looked at his famous friend and said, "You have no idea how much this means to me."

"Your friend, Warren played a huge role in this," Alberto pointed out.

"I believe it," said Peter.

Warren Striker made his way through the crowd and approached Alberto and Peter. "Looks like all three of us scored feeders!" he said.

"And that calls for a group hug," commented Alberto. Three sets of arms emotionally held each another in thanks.

"Peter," said Alberto. "Your feeder is almost the size of a house! My band will use one of our moving vans and deliver it to your place tomorrow."

"Make it around noon," said Peter. "I'll have a barbeque going." Pointing at Warren Striker he said, "And I expect to see you and everybody there!"

"Food? Me?" replied Warren. "I'll be the first one there and help you set up."

"And remember to bring our man, Chase!" said Alberto.

"Who did you think I invited first?" questioned Peter.

The press knew to be at the MCC on Friday and Saturday nights. Immediately questions were being asked with pictures taken.

––––––––––

The following day Warren and Peter were setting up the picnic when a group of five men entered the back yard singing:

"Hi ho, hi ho, it's off to work we go..."

It was the V-O Fives carrying Peter's feeder. They stopped with Rico asking, "Where would you like it?"

Peter knew exactly where he wanted it. Running to the boundary line where his property paralleled the neighboring field he said, "Right here."

The band placed the Meadowdale Feeder where Peter pointed. "I brought something," said Warren. He left and returned minutes later carrying two large bags of bird feed. Handing a bag to Peter, he said. "Let's fill 'er up."

"I'll get the garden hose," said Alberto.

In no time, the feeder was ready for the bird community. Its top half was full of bird seed and the lower half filled with water. Peter grabbed a handful of seed from the top drum and walked into the pasture where Karl lived. He gave his distinct whistle and threw some seed into the air. All at once the sky filled with chirping sounds with a swarm of sparrows flying towards Peter.

Everyone watched.

The man with one eye threw more seed in the air as he walked towards the feeder. Soon the sparrows were pecking the ground with others landing on the monument made of musical instruments.

Off in the distance was an approaching sparrow flying as if it was in a wind storm. A struggling Karl was seen by everyone pulling up the rear. Peter began waving his arms as if to *guide it*. With determination, the tiny bird reached its destination and perched itself on the rim of the top drum. Karl began pecking away at his meal with Peter calling out. "He made it! Karl is eating with the rest; he can now fend for himself!"

A teary-eyed Warren Striker raised his hook and yelled, "Go, Karl, go!"

CHAPTER XXVII

The town of Meadowdale was growing one way and deteriorating in another. The MCC with its popular feeder was definitely a draw. The big picture, however, told a different story. There was no construction taking place in the little town with only demolition crews steadily working. The MCC appeared to be Meadowdale's saving grace, putting all of its marbles in one bag.

Fate was around the corner. This seemingly unsinkable liner was on the verge of crossing paths with an iceberg.

Early Monday morning had county inspectors facing a chore they were hoping to avoid. It took only a few scrapes with a putty knife, a couple pulls from a crowbar and a brief inspection to detect dry rot from stem to stern. The gallant landmark that the world was coming to know was abruptly condemned.

Andy met John and Julia in the parking lot. They stood silent seeing their building painted with squiggly fluorescent lines and barricaded with caution tape. A warning sign posted on the front door ordered 'No Trespassing.'

Andy called Mayor Warren Striker and told him the devastating news. "What? You're kidding me!" replied the man with the shiny hook.

Word spread quickly that the MCC was ruled unsafe with volunteers needed immediately. It was arranged with the county that the community center could be entered to move its contents to the Meadowdale City Hall Auditorium. A rescue operation that involved all who heard of the tragedy. An emergency town meeting was scheduled for the following evening with *everyone* being asked to attend.

———————

Tuesday evening arrived with Chase Mansfield sitting with his mother and uncle. "I'm scared mom," said Chase holding his mother's hand.

"You don't have a thing to worry about," she said in a comforting tone. "Just say prayers and God will answer them."

Chase followed his mother's advice knowing that prayer has never failed him before. In silence, he asked our creator to help the situation by restoring the community center he and his friends called *home*. The boy was even willing to have it replaced, just as long as they *had* one.

The auditorium was packed to the rafters. On center stage was Mayor Striker with specific members from the MCC sitting at a table. The mayor gave an introduction explaining how shocked they were over the closure. From there, he announced that the meeting would be an open floor to allow everyone to express their concerns and offer any suggestions.

It came as no surprise to have Grace Collins voice her complaint first. Whenever there was a petition going around town, she either started it or was the first to sign.

"The community center helped us with those beautiful feeders," she said shaking her index finger. "But we still lost another building despite all that effort. I think we're doomed!"

It seemed that Grace was right. Not one person contested what she said, until Andy Rutledge weighed in...

A frightful minute of silence slowly passed until the mysterious man in the wheelchair made his move. "I have to disagree with you," he said with his baritone voice. Rolling away from the desk, he locked the wheels and stood up. The audience gasped in disbelief.

Chase gave a huge grin as a secure feeling tingled throughout his entire body. The boy always envisioned Andy as Superman and *knew* he could fly.

The room remained silent as Andy began to explain himself. "Everyone here knows me as Andy Rutledge; a member of the MCC. I guess what remained a secret was *why* I came here." Andy began to pace using his hands to gather his thoughts. Finally, he spoke.

"I grew up far away from here in a town just like this one. My father was a hard working man who contracted polio one day. Eventually, he was confined to a wheelchair. My mother and I assisted him in every way possible as he accepted his condition and adjusted to it. He never complained though," Andy pointed out. "In fact, he didn't even ask for anything. He just wanted to be independent and live a life without bothering anyone else. I respected that and dedicated my life to help those who were in my father's situation."

The room was captivated as Andy continued.

"That's why I am often seen in a wheelchair," he said. "I wanted to see people the way my dad did. I also went on to start a business that's called *Good Samaritan Products.* It's one of the world's leading manufacturers for wheelchairs, walkers, canes, hospital beds and anything a disabled person is in need of. At least once a week, I live in one of my products to fully understand the life my customers are forced to live."

There was not one dry eye in the house as Andy spoke further.

"I have heard many good things about this town and its community center," he said. "It was also brought to my attention that Meadowdale had plenty of land for the taking and a spirited workforce waiting to be called upon. Recently, my staff purchased several hundred acres across the street from the MCC. This is to build a state-of-the-art manufacturing complex that will easily employ at least one-hundred people at a good union wage.

The entire room stood up and cheered. The town of Meadowdale had been saved!

Andy was now performing like the CEO he was. "Are there any questions?" he asked.

Chase Mansfield's hand was the first to be raised. "Go ahead, Chase," said Andy.

"Can you do anything about our community center?" he asked. "We need it to build more feeders."

Andy stopped in his tracks. Looking at Chase, he said, "You're right. I will personally see to it that a community center is built on the very ground where our present one stands. I'll even replace the portable that we lost a while ago. The one where *Humphrey* lived." Pointing at Chase he said, "The new community center and its portable will be constructed first and immediately."

At that moment, a familiar figure stood up several feet away from Chase. "The V-O Fives will help finance this project; just tell us how much you need." It was none other then Alberto Ribas in his street clothes supporting the town he learned to love.

Andy grinned as the movement gained support. "Anything else?" he asked the audience.

Chase's hand went up a second time with Andy calling on him.

"Can I ask another question?" he asked.

Andy made a comment. "Chase, as far as I am concerned, you're the smartest person I've ever met. What is it?"

Chase cleared his throat and addressed another potential disaster. "We were told that our community center was just as old as the retirement home and animal shelter. If they have to close down, could new ones be built across the street like your factory?"

Andy was stunned. The writing was on the wall that those homes would be next. He digested Chase's idea and saw the beauty in uniting the three complexes across the street from the *new* MCC.

His business venture would have such people readily available to test out new ideas for the industry.

Transporting seniors to the MCC would be simplified with sky bridges connecting the two properties. Buses would still be guaranteed to help those who needed a little extra.

Consolidating his factory with an updated retirement home and animal shelter was a perfect fit. After all, what senior wouldn't want to walk a dog or have tea with a purring cat on their lap?

With his patented loving smile, Andy addressed Chase. "You are right, again. As CEO of Good Samaritan Products, I promise that those homes will be replaced by new ones. They will be built on the same grounds with my new plant."

Alberto injected a second time. "And the V-O Fives will donate whatever you need for these projects, Brother Andy."

It was arranged that the Meadowdale City Hall Auditorium would house the *homeless* MCC. Its weekly productions and presentations would not miss a beat.

In the meantime, Andy used his assets to quickly get the new community center and portable project underway. True to form, he hired any and all locals who were looking for work.

CHAPTER XXVIII

I t seemed that the town of Meadowdale was playing *Musical Chairs*. The MCC activities once held on the edge of town were now taking place in the heart of Meadowdale. This temporary home for the community center did have its rewards. It was much larger and within walking distance for many. Their open door policy also introduced who they were with everyone encouraged to participate. The oldest institutions that signified the community's first dwellings would soon become their newest.

Across town, the pride continued. Andy Rutledge employed any who needed work. They in turn went the extra mile and restored the original landscape with some additional features. Trails, picnic sites and barbeque pits would once again grace the beautiful campus. Within five months, the new MCC project was complete and ready for a ribbon cutting ceremony. It was agreed that "Mr. Meadowdale Feeder" himself (Chase Mansfield) was deserving of this honor.

It was a beautiful Saturday morning at Meadowdale's newest facility: The Meadowdale Community Center. Thousands were present along with reporters, microphones and TV cameras. Approaching the parking lot one could see the vast improvements. The lot itself was much larger than before with trees, bushes and ferns accenting beautiful rockery.

The main building was a sight to behold. It was constructed of varnished wood with a rock foundation. The structure was considerably bigger than the one it replaced. The old steps were replaced with inclines to assist those using wheelchairs. Walkways outlined with street lamps led to several entryways with manicured trails leading different directions throughout the grounds.

This acreage was once again the prime real-estate of Meadowdale.

Mayor Warren Striker stood with Chase Mansfield in front of the main doors. He held a large pair of scissors and gave a brief speech crediting Chase's efforts.

"Chase Mansfield brought new life to the MCC, and to the town of Meadowdale as a whole."

The crowd cheered as his mother cried over her son's recognition. Behind him was a thick red ribbon. The mayor handed him the scissors with Chase cutting the ribbon in one clip.

Another ovation erupted from the masses.

The new facility was declared open with Chase and Warren Striker being the first to enter. Once inside the ambiance of the new complex took control. The lobby was surrounded with wooden walls that matched the outside of the building. Beams made of polished logs ran diagonal from floor to ceiling in contrast with striking red molding.

There was more.

The history of the MCC wasn't forgotten. Pieces of white concrete walls that displayed hand prints throughout the years were embedded sporadically down every hallway.

The journey through the new MCC was a venture all in its own. Upon entering the main lobby and to the left was a vastly improved homeroom. It was twice the size as the one it replaced, with a full-size kitchen attached. New chairs and tables blanket the polished wooden floors.

To enter the lobby and go straight, one would find a cafeteria large enough to feed an army. To the right was a hallway that had doors leading to two enormous arts and crafts rooms. At the end of the hall was an auditorium larger than the one at city hall. It was luxurious like its predecessor, with an added bonus.

The back of the stage had a roll up door that converted it into an amphitheater. This outside section of the building had a Roman-style courtyard with curved seating made of granite. It even had huge pillars resembling the ancient coliseum for total effect. This assured that massive crowds could watch the MCC presentations regardless of numbers. Grassy slopes offered 'picnic style' seating if needed.

As always, plenty of restrooms, benches and plants accompanied the structure with an industrial-size loading dock tucked away.

The Main building was not the only attraction. There were lavish grounds to explore and a replacement for an old portable to be toured. A place where a maimed squirrel lived not too long ago...

———————

The *squirrel patrol* had been nursing bruised egos for months. A recent reunion brought forth a revelation that re-created who they *really* were. "We're not savages," pointed out John. "That pertains to species lower on the food chain."

"You're right," agreed Steve. "Why, we're not hunters at all; we are too civilized for that."

"We most certainly are," commented Allen.

The men reached the conclusion that they were *not* food gathers. They were *home finders*.

"I'm so relieved to learn of this," said John brushing the back of his hand against his forehead.

They helped with Andy's MCC project and had the corner of the new art room planted exactly where the old one stood. Using a spade and garden hoe, they dug a hole identical to the one 'Humphrey' called *home*. Next, 'Sparkles' was positioned and secured where the electric meter once stood.

Julia went to their car and brought the caged rodent to her son. "Why did you bring Humphrey here?" he asked.

"Chase, we have a big surprise for you and Humphrey," said the mother. "One that I know you'll both love."

"Really?" asked the teen.

"Really," she replied.

Peter Constantine and Warren Striker were within hearing range and wanted to see what Julia was talking about. She was suddenly approached by her brother, John, and the father and son team of Steve and Allen Smith. "Are we ready?" asked John.

"We're ready," answered Julia.

With cage in hand, they walked towards the trail that led to the new art building. Seeing the family together with the caged pet drew everyone's attention as they followed. They walked the short path that led to the pasture where Chase fed Humphrey. There before them stood a smaller replica of the MCC's main building. It, too, was a wooden structure with a rock foundation. Wide ramps that matched the building's exterior led to its front and back doors. It was another work of art that gave three times the space as the one before.

Chase gazed in amazement to see such a majestic creation gracing the pasture like a fairytale story.

At that moment, his heart started to flutter. He noticed Sparkles smiling at him. He knew that the Martian-type feeder was there to guide Humphrey home. The boy nodded over and over again at the friendly alien, knowing that he accomplished his mission. "Mom," said Chase. "Sparkles wants Humphrey to come home now. It's okay," he continued. "I will always visit them and keep Sparkles full."

Warren and Peter caught every word the boy said. They were always mystified over that special person named, Chase Mansfield. Many times when they visited over coffee his name was mentioned. There was something about him they were able to relate to. Something ever-present that they couldn't quite put a finger on.

Julia handed the cage to her son and kept quiet. Chase walked towards Sparkles and was delighted to see that 'he' was already serviced with peanuts and water. Kneeling down he gave the pet what it always wanted. It's freedom.

The squirrel leaped out of the cage, pranced towards its residential numbers and stopped. An obvious precaution to make sure 'he' was at the right address.

Warren and Peter knew of the wild pet, but have never actually looked at it. For the first time, they saw the squirrel and realized that it was deformed. Immediately it hit them like a cold slap in the face. Slowly, they turned and stared at each other with words not needed. At that precise moment, it dawned on them what it was about Chase Mansfield that always held their attention: *He was one of them.*

Humphrey seemed to verify that those were indeed the right numbers to his home. He also appeared to acknowledge Sparkles. Like 'Elsie' the lion, he raced across the grass and climbed into his hole.

"He's probably not hungry now because I fed him this morning," commented Chase.

CHAPTER XXIX

The festivities taking place that Saturday were not limited to the new MCC. At 12:00 noon, a groundbreaking ceremony would be taking place across the street.

Andy Rutledge wore a bright orange construction hat as he thrust a shovel into the dirt. Scooping it up he received cheers from the audience. He was on live camera with pictures being taken. When asked how he felt he answered:

"Meadowdale is the right town for anyone to set up shop." Andy Rutledge was well known throughout many investment institutions. His words would entice future business ventures.

Mayor Striker stood next to Andy with the press asking him a few questions. "You must be proud of this town," commented a reporter.

"Oh, I am," replied Warren Striker. "Everyone here is helping every step of the way."

Peter Constantine was present and recognized as a mayoral candidate. The reporter asked him a question. "Peter, how is your campaign developing?"

That question took Warren by surprise. Long ago he forgot that his friend, Peter, was also his political opponent. "It's a sure win for our camp," said Peter with confidence.

Warren felt disowned by that comment until he heard the rest.

"That's because I'm not running against Mayor Striker, I'm running with him," said the man with a Bavarian accent. "I don't care what party we run as or what position I'll actually have. All I care about is supporting our mayor, Warren Striker. I'll even volunteer if necessary." Peter leaned over Warren and put his arm around his shoulder. "This town is fortunate to have him."

Warren was taken by his friend's loyalty. The press placed the microphone in front of the incumbent. "I can't do anything without Peter Constantine," he said, placing his arm around Peter's shoulder. "The good things that are happening around here are a direct result of Peter's involvement."

Striker and Constantine: A political party destined to take care of the town of Meadowdale.

Andy Rutledge had a keen sense for business and believed in the town of Meadowdale. His initial move caused a well thought out domino theory. The following week more property was purchased by corporations. A nationally acclaimed log home manufacturer bought a hundred acres to build their latest plant, bringing in more jobs. Two hotel chains established territory in the quaint town followed by three all-purpose gas stations. The restaurant industry made their presence known with a few well-known conglomerates springing up. Local ventures followed suit by opening up their kitchens.

Across the street, things were rock'n! More and more people were dropping by to see what the MCC was all about and to *experience Meadowdale.* On occasion, a new face wearing a monogrammed shirt would be spotted. Somewhere, someone placed a non-offensive donation box just inside the lobby. It became very popular yielding funds that further supported the center.

The facility was a state park in its own right. The many picnic tables, barbeques, trails, ponds and gardens were an open invitation for families to spend the day. As always, the MCC started its day with 'social time' with all invited. This gave one the opportunity to meet the famous Chase Mansfield and his many friends, enjoy refreshments and pet an overly affectionate golden retriever.

That morning, Ruth Watson arrived bringing homemade chocolate chip cookies. The African American woman from generations ago brought another special treat: her younger sister, Maggie, her aunt, Teresa and a childhood friend named, Sue. "This is the most wonderful place I know of," she explained as she parked her car. Getting out of the vehicle, she opened the trunk to get a folded wheelchair and walker. Her aunt was confined to the chair, with her sister needing the walker.

"Are you sure they won't mind us visiting?" asked her Aunt Teresa.

"Mind?" questioned Ruth. "This place is full of people just like you. They'll love you!" she promised.

How right she was. Ruth led them to the homeroom where other wheelchairs and walkers waited. Teresa, Maggie and Sue knew they were accepted.

Looking at the three women Ruth said, "Well just don't stand there; c'mon on in and introduce yourself!"

———————

The community center was a non-stop social hour with many friends and feeders being made. It all came to a head on Friday and Saturday nights when the famous presentations took over.

The auditorium and outside seating was always full when the show started. The play and ballets were modified from time to time, but always left the audience wanting more. The contestants and their Meadowdale feeders were always unpredictable.

Bwwaaaam! A Meadowdale Feeder made out of cooking utensils for a retired army cook.

Bwwaaaam! A Meadowdale Feeder made out of sports paraphernalia for a retired coach.

Bwwaaam! A Meadowdale Feeder made out of an old sewing machine and crochet needles for a grandmother turning eighty.

Bwwwaaaammmmm! A Meadowdale Feeder made out of a childhood tricycle for a man who turned one hundred.

Somewhere away in the distant suburbs a revolt was taking place.

"Hamilton, my darling, I'm getting bored."

Mr. Belvedeere was perplexed. The late model male with silver hair just emptied their last can of silly string. Something had to be done with almost the entire day ahead of them. "Lovey, do you want me to call the skipper and schedule another cruise?"

The elegant woman wearing a silk outfit with pearls replied. "No darling, he has a propensity for getting lost."

Walking towards the window, an exciting thought entered her mind. "I know," she said. Turning around, she faced her husband. "Let's go to Meadowdale and meet that wonderful boy, Chase Mansfield."

Hamilton followed her way of thinking. "Do you mean that it's time for us to experience Meadowdale?"

Extending her arms she hugged the man saying, "Yes, I've heard so much about it."

"Splendid!" he replied.

Within moments, they were off to Meadowdale with 'James' chauffeuring. "I do think this will be entertaining," she commented.

The Belvedeeres soon found themselves on the MCC campus. There were many walking around with an air of happiness about. "Why, everybody's here," said Hamilton in a befuddled tone. The wealthy man felt awkward that such an event never reached out to his social circle.

"It's like the Mardi Gras!" exclaimed his wife. Looking at her husband, she said in disbelief, "And nobody gave us a personal invitation?"

This was a crisis. They were members of the upper-crust and considered their social circle as *the aristocrats of the state.* If anyone were to know about this, it should have been *them* first.

Mrs. Belvedeere saw a middle-aged man with a shiny hook. "Look, Hamilton. It's that brave war hero that runs this town."

Warren Striker was two steps ahead of them. The moment he caught the fragrance of Chanel No. 5 mixed with two other exotic perfumes, he smelled a car sell.

Approaching the couple, he gave that first impression that could only be made once. He acted star-struck. With hands at his side, he tensed up with bulging eyes. Taking a step backwards he pretended to be caught off guard saying, "You're here!"

His professionalism worked like the charm. The Belvedeeres immediately took a liking to him and *introduced themselves* out of etiquette. That's all Striker Motors had to know.

Peter saw the immediate exchange. He generally didn't approve of Warren's survival skills, but greatly appreciated them when applied properly. The trio sat at a nearby bench with Mrs. Belvedeere initiating a conversation. "We do find those feeders that the community center makes so fascinating," she said.

"Yes," said Warren. "We're all proud of that." Speaking under his breath he added, "But that's not where the gold mine is..."

Hamilton interpreted Warren's comment the way it was meant. It was obviously a discrete tip on the local stock market. "Tell me more," he asked.

Warren's eyes kept scanning their surroundings as he was about to reveal a well-kept secret. "The feeders are doing okay, but it's the Meadowdale Art that's should really skyrocket."

"Meadowdale Art?" asked Mrs. Belvedeere.

Placing his index finger in front of his mouth, he made the *please be quiet sound.* "Shhhhhh. I don't want this to get out to the wrong people," he whispered.

Mrs. Belvedeere's shoulders raised as her face showed excitement. It was a thrill acting like an agent undercover. "Okay," she whispered.

The Belvedeeres sat closer as Warren spoke. We're proud of our feeders, but they are created by what's brought in. The artwork is an entirely different story. They are truly how our members express themselves with no restrictions. That's why I haven't sold any to the public yet. I don't think anyone around here could appreciate what they really are."

Hamilton took the bait. "Can we see them?" he asked.

"Sure," said Warren. "Just act casual when someone walks by."

Mrs. Belvedeere was getting giddy. She played with her fingers, getting mentally prepared. "Okay," she whispered with a child's grin on her face.

The trio was soon in the MCC art room looking at the many paintings, sketches and watercolors displayed about. "They're incredible!" said Mr. Belvedeere.

He was right.

Each hanging displayed a personal touch from the artist. This ranged from the plight their lives consisted of, to their Godly appreciation of people and nature. Some pieces were abstract, but delivered their message while others exploded with colors, waiting to be framed for a mantel piece.

Mrs. Belvedeere looked all directions. "They're beautiful!" she exclaimed.

Peter entered the room without the Belvedeeres noticing. "Tell, me," asked Hamilton. "How can one buy these incredible works?"

Warren was in his element. Leaning off to the side he rolled his eyes saying, "Well, I don't know... I plan on sending out special invitations to rent out the MCC for one night and allow those present to make bids.

Instinctively, he pulled out his checkbook with pen in hand. "And how much would that be?"

Warren had his fish on the line and played it perfectly. He implied that it might be too much for them. "You might not want to get involved with this, it will cost a pretty penny."

Human nature set in with Hamilton accepting the challenge. "How much?" he asked.

Peter was amused and acted like a prizefighter being beat to the canvas. An impersonation that only his friend could see. Quickly he left the room as to not jeopardize the sale.

"I like to honor our guests by letting them make an offer," replied the mayor.

Mr. Belvedeere put his best foot forward and wrote down a handsome figure. Handing the check to Warren he asked, "Is this enough?"

Warren's hands trembled when he saw the amount. "That will be plenty," he said.

It was arranged for the inaugural Meadowdale Art Auction to take place the following Wednesday evening at seven. This gave both parties ample time to prepare. Mayor Warren Striker gave the couple a grand tour then took them out for dinner. Later, he contacted Peter and coordinated a meeting with the MCC hierarchy. The following day the mayor was at the community center with Peter, Andy, Renée and the others who coordinated activities.

"Their artwork is another venture that already has a demand," said Warren. He displayed the check made out to the MCC. "Look," he said. "They loved what they saw and want to be a part of this. It's just the beginning!"

"I think it's a brilliant idea," said Andy. "It's a good feeling seeing that everything the members put out becomes gold."

"I agree," said Julia Mansfield. "The more involvement we have, the more help the community gets."

"This is like the Governor's Day Celebration we had a while back," said Warren. "If we really put on a show for these people, they'll want more."

"I agree," said Steve.

"I'll arrange a wine and cheese party with a string quintet," said Renée "I will also see to it that our dining room is well decorated with plenty of fresh flowers."

"I'll help you with that," said Julia.

The committee was in full support of having the 'elite' involved. The partaking of a wine and cheese social with a silent auction would prove to be highly successful.

"It's important to bring Chase," pointed out Warren. "The Belvedeeres told me that they and all of their friends fell in love with him."

CHAPTER XXX

Wednesday evening arrived with BMWs, Jaguars, Rolls-Royces and other status symbols parked at the MCC. The elite had arrived in Meadowdale and they were wearing their formals.

It was agreed that Chase Mansfield would wear his jeans and traditional bright red MCC shirt with his name printed on it.

The reasoning? That's how the press and 'TV-land' introduced him to their culture. A different kind of Ronald McDonald.

The young star, accompanied by his mother, uncle and Mayor Striker approached the facility. The upper crust was ready with a woman of distinction posed by the main doors. Her dyed auburn hair was glorified with a diamond necklace and matching earrings. A brand name floral dress perfectly matched the high-heels she wore, making her look exquisite. The night's gentle breeze assured that this woman needed no introduction. It was Mrs. Belvedeere.

"Oh, Chase my darling, it's so good to see you..."

Without warning, John coughed with Julia making an involuntary swaying motion with her arm. The welcome wagon knew that it was going to be a long evening.

"Please come in, my dear and introduce me to your friends."

They entered the MCC and were immediately flocked by the county's *who's who*. Tuxedos, mink stoles, jewelry and currents of imported perfume were all waiting. John and Julia were introduced as Chase's family and received massive hugs of respect. The drawing card, however, was to meet the flamboyant man with the shiny hook, and especially Chase Mansfield. The brother and sister team faded into the background and watched the challenged boy with the capacity of an eight-year-old hobnob with the upper class.

His sincere blue eyes honored each and every person who spoke with him. He was obviously happy to be there appreciating all he met. Several feet away was the trademark hook swinging in the air as the art of 'one-upmanship' was underway.

Renée and Andy were 'busy as a bee' in the kitchen. A subtle 'clearing of the throat' sound caught her attention as she turned around. It was Mr. Belvedeere expressing that he felt his money was well spent. A wink that only a cagey tycoon could deliver was addressed to her. She smiled back appreciating the recognition.

Renée Klause did double duty burning the midnight oil for this event. Her famous floral displays graced the entire room including each table. Candles were placed strategically with a breathtaking indoor waterfall rented for the center of the room. Domestic and imported wine, crackers and cheeses were served by professional servers that dressed like *5ᵗʰ Avenue*. A Neapolitan string quintet matched the elegance, not missing a beat.

Most of all, the lovable Chase Mansfield was there for everybody.

The boy who invented the first Meadowdale Feeder was 'tic for tac' with laughing, listening and sharing. Soon he raised his head above the crowd and asked, "Would anyone like to see the community center with me?"

All were takers.

"I'd love to!"

"Why that's a wonderful idea!"

"Splendid!"

"Let's do it!"

Chase Mansfield had an ace up his sleeve. It was rehearsed earlier in the week for him to keep an eye on his mother during the social. When she made a certain hand motion, he was to call out to the entire room and make such a suggestion.

Chase led the patrons down the hall and approached the main art room. He nonchalantly gave a distinct knock on the door and paused a moment. In a gentlemanly fashion, he opened the door to let his guest enter first.

Hamilton Belvedeere, his wife and friends walked into an unexpected barrage of cheers.

"Surprise!"

Inside was the remainder of the MCC membership, a guaranteed spice for their evening! It was East meeting West, with introductions, handshakes and hugs exchanged. The room broke into small conversations with interesting tidbits of information and trivia being passed about.

This was an eye-opener for those of the highest tax bracket. The very types of people who were forbidden to wash their cars, do lawn care or set foot on their property were represented here. It was immediately understood that the MCC members were a collective group of compassionate souls, ones who weren't a detriment to society and had plenty to show for their lives.

Chase Mansfield was approached by Ralph Rollings, a prominent fashion designer. "Chase, would you mind showing us how you do some of your art projects?"

"Sure," he said.

He went to a cabinet and grabbed two standard sized sheets of paper used for finger painting. Next he pointed at a rack that held over fifty jars of paint. "If anyone here has a favorite color, go ahead and pick it out," he said. Mrs. Kirkpatrick was closest and grabbed the colors forest green, aqua blue and orange.

Everyone watched the artistic genius pour a dab of each color on one sheet. Without a thought, he dipped his fingertips in the orange paint and gently swiped the bare canvas.

"Oooooo," was the pulsating response from the guests.

Chase looked at Mrs. Kirkpatrick and asked, "Would you like to help?"

Maureen Kirkpatrick was a trooper. The sixty-four-year-old real-estate mogul grew up with three brothers. Camping, fishing and getting her hands dirty was her upbringing. She took off her priceless rings and ran a set of fingers through the aqua blue paint. With finesse, she brushed her fingers like an alpha wave across Chase's stroke.

Like a duet with Paul Simon, she was composing a work of art with non-other then Chase Mansfield himself.

The colorful array was finally finished with Chase doing something he always did. He wrote his name on the bottom corner. The upper crust watched, learning what to look for when bidding on *Meadowdale Art.*

"We need to let it dry now," said the artist with curly blonde hair. "Then you can take it home."

Maureen placed both arms around the boy with her fingers extended as to not spread wet paint. "Thank you, Chase," she said.

"You're welcome," he replied. Addressing the room he offered,"Would anyone else like to make a painting?"

Many answers came back at once.

"I do!"

"I'd love to, Chase!"

"Can I?"

"Sure!"

Chase felt successful and blushed. "My friends are really good at this and will help anyone paint a good picture," he said.

Soon it was art class with *new members* being shown the ropes. Everyone who arrived for wine and cheese that evening took home a special *Meadowdale*. A priceless *Rembrandt* they personally created with help from Chase Mansfield and his friends.

Looking at the MCC members was a rude awakening. It was one that addressed their flawed belief about a *separation of classes*. To some, it really hit home as a wake-up call. It was time to reach out to a distant family member, neighbor or grocery clerk who was long-overdue for acceptance.

Hamilton walked by Mayor Striker and whispered into his ear. "It's a good idea to empty the donation box by the front door so we can fill it again."

Hamilton and his friends could go anywhere in the world at a snap of a finger. Still, their search for happiness continued until they discovered the MCC. It took their surprise visit to the art room to finally find what they were always looking for: *fun!*

It was time to go back to the makeshift ballroom with the silent auction being set up. A motivated clientele was fired up with checkbooks in hand.

The following morning found the MCC graced with baskets of flowers, candy and fruits. It was accompanied with a large 'thank you' card signed by everyone who attended last night's auction. Andy was sitting with Chase, his mother and a few others. He asked the boy a question.

"How did you like Mr. and Mrs. Belvedeere and their friends last night?"

"They were very nice to me," answered Chase.

"I bet they were," said Andy.

"Andy, can I ask you a question?" asked Chase.

"Sure," came his response.

"I noticed that those people talk differently than we do," commented Chase.

"What do you mean?" he asked.

"Well..." said Chase as he began to gather his thoughts. "They always do *this* with their hand when they say, "Hi," to each other." Chase stood up and extended his arm with an open hand, then dropped his fingers once his arm was fully extended.

"Oh, *that*," commented Andy.

Chase sat down and elaborated further. "They also call each other, "Dear" and take turns mentioning different countries they just visited." With a confused look on his face he asked, "Why do they do that?"

Andy started to digest the question. Looking around he saw, Steve, John, Julia and Renée waiting to hear the answer.

Turning to Chase he said, "No one really knows why they do that."

Chase accepted his answer and had one last burning question. "Can I ask you another question?"

"Go right ahead," said Andy.

"What's *Grey Poupon?*"

CHAPTER XXXI

The following year had the factory across the street up and running. The retirement home and animal shelter were also in full swing. Their grounds rivaled the MCC with acres of green grass, trails and picnic sites. Equally important, they too offered fun-filled tours. Sky bridges linked the properties together with people constantly coming and going.

The seniors that were once dying of loneliness now had a different situation. It was common practice for those experiencing Meadowdale to freely walk into the new retirement home and recruit a resident for dinner. Their widely-known involvement with the MCC generated a fanfare of autograph hounds with group pictures high on the list. If anyone from the Meadowdale Retirement Home wanted company or an offer to go out for dinner, all they had to do was to be seen in plain sight and wait...

These seniors were active to say the least. They lived between a thriving factory and a modern animal shelter. Throughout the week, workers would contact their neighbors next door to extend yet another invitation to a potluck, buffet or barbeque. There were even times when Andy Rutledge would contact the home and ask for volunteers to test his latest products.

On the other side existed the new Meadowdale Animal Shelter. It too was a lively place open to the public. Pets were continuously *borrowed* and taken out for the day. The popular Experience Meadowdale Package recommended visiting the shelter and allowing *any animal to adopt you.* Any except for a crazy talking bird that had an understanding with Mayor Warren Striker. *Bbrrraakk!*

The town as a whole was flourishing as well. Businesses backed by major corporations got established in the festive community with more on the way. It also offered its seclusion with many buying properties a few miles from town and building cabins. There were even internationally acclaimed celebrities that had summer homes built in Meadowdale. Utilizing a low profile, they enjoyed blending in with the locals.

The entire town was holding its own, but nothing compared to the MCC on Fridays and Saturdays. The indoor/outdoor presentation was always packed with the audience going insane.

Bwaaaam! A Meadowdale Feeder made of an old hair dryer with scissors, combs and curling irons for a retired beautician.

Bwaaaam! A Meadowdale Feeder made of a vintage typewriter with pens, pencils and reading glasses for an author's retirement.

Bwaaaam! A Meadowdale Feeder made of fishing poles, nets and lures hanging like Christmas tree ornaments for another retiree.

Bwwaaaaammmm! A Meadowdale Feeder made from a bicycle frame, handlebars, tire rims and bike helmets for a son's graduation.

The MCC's popularity continued to grow with more and more families choosing to vacation in the quaint town. Even game shows were awarding Experience Meadowdale Packages. Meadow Feeder clubs also began to spring up with their own monthly publications.

One could only pity the household of a Meadowdale Feeder going through a divorce...

——— ——— ———

One day a special visitor came to town to conduct business with Chase Mansfield. He arrived in a black limousine accompanied by his staff. His name: Hershel Vincent Graham IV.

The distinguished man looked like a sea captain from the last century. His weathered face was masterfully groomed with silver hair and a matching beard. He wore a black suit with gold buttons. The white shirt and conservative silver and blue tie came right out of a movie.

He entered the MCC and happened across Julia Mansfield. Graciously, the seventy-one year-old-man with piercing blue eyes called out to her.

"Excuse me, madam; I was hoping to find a Mr. Chase Mansfield."

Julia was stunned. The regal man with an entourage in three piece suits was obviously on an important assignment.

"He's my son," she answered.

"Jolly good!" he responded. "My name is, Hershel Vincent Graham IV," he said with his charm. Extending his hand he asked, "And you are?"

"Julia Mansfield," she said with a cute curtsey. "Pleased to meet you."

Hershel was amused and laughingly said, "The pleasure's mine."

"I came here to address your son about an important business matter," said Hershel. "Perhaps you could join us."

"Are you aware of his condition?" asked the protective mother.

"We know everything about him," remarked Hershel. "And we greatly respect that boy."

John was seen walking down the hall with Julia identifying him. Pointing at him, she said, "That's my brother over there. He is my son's father figure since his real father left us a long time ago."

"Let's include him," suggested the business man.

They were introduced and found a nearby vacant room. While opening up the door, they came across Warren Striker joyfully pushing Andy Rutledge in his wheelchair.

Julia greeted them and began to introduce Warren and Andy.

"I know who you are," said Hershel Vincent Graham IV. "You're that charismatic mayor the entire country is talking about!" He gently grabbed Warren's hook and shook it.

Mayor Warren Striker loved how Hershel gave him recognition. Their names were exchanged with Andy included. "We might as well stay together since you're all close to Chase."

"Okay," said Julia. "I'll go get him."

The men entered the room along with Hershel's associates and sat at a table. Soon Julia returned with her son.

Immediately, Hershel got up and walked over to Chase. With both hands extended he leaned forward saying, "Chase, my name is Hershel Vincent Graham IV." The boy shook his hands saying, "My name is Chase Mansfield; please to meet you."

The three men that accompanied Hershel were formally introduced, with everybody having met everyone. Hershel sat back down and took charge. "Chase," he said. "People all over the country know who you are, and they love those pet feeders you invented."

Chase sat up with a huge grin on his face. He looked at his mom and saw how proud she was. "In fact," said Hershel. "We believe that the whole world wants one and that's why I'm here."

That comment caught everyone's attention.

"My firm is one of the most reputable investment firms out of New York," he said. "We only work with what we consider to be a *high clientele*." Looking at Julia, he asked, "Are you his legal guardian?"

Julia tensed up a bit wondering what he was aiming at. "Yes I am."

"Good, good," responded the tycoon.

"I still let my son have a say in matters that concern him," she added.

The man in the black suit loved what he heard. With confidence, he began his pitch. Looking at Chase Mansfield the big wheel addressed him further. "Chase, I'm going to make you a rich man if you accept our offer."

At that moment, he opened his blazer and presented a check to the boy. "Please show this to your mother and let me know what you think." The investor then looked at one of his aides and gave a slight motion. Immediately, a contract was handed to him with it being placed on the table. He took an expensive gold plated pen out of his pen pocket and placed it next to the documents.

Chase and his mother looked at the check and were astounded over the many zeros that followed the first number. Julia's eyebrows raised in disbelief with Chase believing it was *all the money in the world.*

"What do you want?" asked Julia.

Leaning back in his chair, the investment mogul gave his answer. "The rights to the Meadowdale Feeder."

That answer went over Chase's head, but Mayor Warren Striker *knew* what that meant. So did the others present.

"What do you mean?" asked Chase.

Hershel Vincent Graham IV relaxed and came down to Chase's intellect. Placing his elbows on the table, he pressed his fingertips together. Using a non-threatening tone, he smiled and began to explain the situation in layman's terms.

"Chase, when one works as hard as you did a reward follows."

That statement confused the boy as he continued to listen.

"What my firm is offering you creates a situation where you will never have to work again. You can now play for the rest of your life." Hershel gave a clown-like smile while nodding his head. An attempt to guide the youth.

Chase was further confused. In his world, *work* and *play* were the same thing.

"You're going to be a rich man, Chase Mansfield."

It was another strike. *Rich* was not a part of Chase Mansfield's vocabulary. He understood what money was and knew that it only pertained to grown-ups like his mother and uncle.

"I still don't understand what you're talking about," said Chase.

"All we want to do is buy the rights to your feeders. This is so that we can build them and use the name, *Meadowdale Feeder*; that's all."

Chase liked his explanation, or so he thought...

"Do you mean that you have people where you come from who are just like us?"

"Why, yes we do," said Hershel. "We have plenty."

"Can I visit them and help them make feeders and do artwork?" asked the boy.

"They won't be building any feeders, Chase. We will have factories full of grownups that will be doing that, and they'll do a great job producing many every day. Soon, Meadowdale Feeders will be in stores everywhere worldwide."

Chase had a follow-up question. "Can those people come over here and play with us and make feeders?"

"Not to make feeders," said Hershel. "We want you and your mother to sign a contract that gives our firm the exclusive rights to build Meadowdale Feeders; with everyone else expressively prohibited."

"Does that mean that we can't build them anymore?" asked Chase.

"That's right," answered Hershel.

Chase became horrified. Looking at the investor, he began to hear the eerie organ music that the old black and white horror movies played. Shows he was forbidden to watch. Hershel's weathered face lost its friendly expression and began to appear evil.

"No," protested Chase. "I don't want to do that! I want to be with my friends and build feeders like Sparkles.

Round one was over with the cagey New Yorker upping the ante. Reaching into his blazer, he pulled out a second check and held it in front of the mother and son. This one had a larger number followed by many zeros.

Chase saw the figure and was alarmed. He knew that the rich man was determined to *steal* the Meadowdale Feeders from the MCC and would have no part of it. Intense blue eyes seemed to penetrate Chase's soul as the organ music got louder. "No, I don't want that!" he cried out.

The friendly tempo of the meeting had definitely taken a turn for the worse. Hershel pulled out his final ace: a third check that tripled the original offer. Chase refused to look at it. "No, go away!" he called out.

The music persisted with the penetrating eyes attempting to control the famous boy.

Hershel backed off and returned to a more friendly demeanor. He re-approached his would-be client in a polite tone. "Chase, you are considered the owner of a product that can make millions happy."

That comment did not go well with him. In his heart, he considered the entire MCC the owner of the Meadowdale Feeder.

The boy looked at Mayor Striker and said, "Isn't this something *all of us* own?"

Warren's hook patted an alarmed Chase on the back. "That's how I always looked at it."

Andy commented, "I agree."

"So do I," said John

"Me, too!" said Julia.

Hershel volleyed back fast. "Chase, there's nothing to be alarmed about. If you sign this contract; the entire world will have Meadowdale Feeders and you won't have to do a thing."

That remark was a huge nail in Hershel's coffin. Chase *wanted* to build more feeders. What was more important; he wanted to do it with his friends.

Looking at mayor Striker, Chase made an *executive decision*. "Can you get a contract I can sign so that the feeders stay right here with our friends?"

It was a perfect idea! The mayor leaned back with a tingling sensation all over his body. "I can draw one up real quick and have your mother review it."

"And we'll sign it," said Julia as she hugged her emotionally distraught son.

Hershel tried one final attempt. "But Chase, you'll be able to buy anything you want."

"No," yelled the boy. "I don't want you, go away!"

It was a long flight back home with Hershel Vincent Graham IV returning empty handed. The man who always rated as one of the world's most successful investors rarely fell short. He mulled over and over again the recent meeting he had at the MCC while scratching his head. Finally, it occurred to him what happened. When it came to buying Chase Mansfield, it was impossible.

He was already wealthy and not for sale.

Chase Mansfield's invention was clearly a reflection of himself.

The very discarded pieces of frayed wires, wrinkled aluminum and glass that the MCC rummaged through personified their image to society. It was as if the original MCC was just a final dumping ground with Chase and his friends considered part of the refuse. The members of the community saw themselves through the scraps. They knew that there was an inner beauty and gave it a second life. One that was more meaningful.

These beautiful creations illustrated how much they respected themselves and cared for others. The famous Meadowdale Feeder in-particular helped display their unconditional love by spreading compassion far and wide. This created a sense of pride for those who called Meadowdale their home. A once depressed community that now had many wearing t-shirts praising the humble town.

The spirit Chase Mansfield and his friends were known for spread in epidemic proportions. It reached out far giving recognition to their old and disadvantaged. A hidden sector that could now express their thoughts, feelings and values through exotic works of art. Lonely souls that were no longer forgotten with many reaching towards them to make a new friend. A friendship that would give a better understanding about life.

Their mission to have others accepted continued to travel. It became common knowledge that anyone who didn't have family was always welcomed to live in Meadowdale. A new 'law of the land' fueled by compassion with a message of good will reaching hearts everywhere. This movement would prove to go a step further. A very important step that motivated Chase Mansfield to create the very first Meadowdale Feeder.

It would touch the lives of Humphrey, Maxwell, Karl and all of their friends.

The End

EPILOGUE

C hase Mansfield and The Meadowdale Community Center represent all of us. They were *easily* chastised for their outward appearance of being handicapped and labeled a detriment to society. A rating system designed and used by those whose deficiencies were hidden on the inside.

This would prove to be a self-gratifying advancement for those who *personally* interpreted such defects as flaws, placing them into categories. A tactic that would inadvertently give oneself a higher rating in the social structure.

Chase and his friends were conveniently set aside on the outskirts of town like the scraps rudely dropped off at their loading dock. It was a 'like attracts like' affair with pallets of material deemed obsolete, begging for a second life.

That's where the tide turned.

This community of humble souls believed in our Creator and knew that the best things in this world were *free*.

With dignity, they accepted this challenge by renovating the thrown out treasures of yesterday and reintroducing them back into the very lives that abandoned them. A second coming that greatly surpassed the joy it initially gave. It was also an indirect statement from the Meadowdale Community Center about life and acceptance others.

Matt Shea

People far and wide challenged this community of *the forgotten and disadvantaged*, asking them to restore what once made them happy. A process that required a trip to the MCC and seeing who these people really were. This introduction opened the eyes of their worse critics and brought down the wall. It resulted in a humble reevaluation for those who formed a conclusion about others who appeared to be weak.

In regards to their famous Meadowdale Feeder, a question arises:

Who were Chase and the members of the MCC *actually* feeding?

ABOUT THE AUTHOR

Matt and his daughter, Laura.

Matt Shea is a developing author having published six books. He is greatly inspired by the writings of Andy Griffith and focuses on the common folk that small towns are made of.

He credits the success of his first book, *The Groundskeeper And Other Short Stories,* to his family. The values that were instilled throughout his childhood gave him the strong sense of justice that is conveyed through his writings. The Shea family is only an average American family from an average neighborhood. Their secret was that they were close-knit and accepted others.

Matt's mother, Vyerl set an example of being self sacrificing; having never placed herself first. She always cared about the feelings of others, no matter who they were. She even sponsored many foster children despite having a family of eight. During the holidays, the Roman Catholic mom would also have a Hanukkah bush for their Jewish friends. There were years when the family would make Christmas gifts and personally deliver them to seniors in rest homes.

The very table that Matt writes all of his stories on came from a childhood neighbor, Netta Wilson. Through time, Netta had to be relocated to assisted living due to deteriorating health. Vyerl never forgot that she and Netta traveled to see the Vatican together. Care packages, visits, and transporting Netta to spend Sundays at their home, became a ritual until her last day. When she passed away, Matt was bequeathed an antique table from Netta. A priceless heirloom that he regards as sacred.

Many of Matt's friends are senior citizens or foreign born. He has the common practice of brewing a pot of tea and inviting them over to watch Alfred Hitchcock. Together they will watch Alfred, share a cup of tea, and afterwards listen to his manuscripts. Sometimes these social gatherings last well beyond midnight. "This is where I get most of my ideas," says Matt. "I learned this from my mom."

Matt Shea appreciates all who take the time to read his stories. He loves feedback and offers his email address for any comments or suggestions you might have. Matt promises to do his very best to answer all who write him. His goal is to reach out to his audience and improve as a writer and a person.

worknmatt7@aol.com